NOT LONG NOW

NOT LONG NOW

John Thomas

Twin Books

Written in 2008 and first published,
by Twin Books, in 2012

© John Thomas 2012

All rights reserved.

ISBN: 978-0-9534304-7-5

The moral right of the author has been asserted.

A Cataloguing in Publication Record
for this title is available from the British Library.

Front cover illustration by Michele Clare
(www.artofimagination.org/pages/clare.html)

Maps reproduced by permission of Ordance Survey on
behalf of HMSO © Crown copyright 2011. All rights
reserved. Ordnance Survey Licence number 100052113.

Typeset in New Baskerville
Made & printed in Great Britain
by SupaPrint (Redditch) Ltd.

TWIN BOOKS
PO Box 3667
WV3 9XZ UK

www.twinbooks.co.uk

By John Thomas:

Beyond This Wilderness
The Welsh Dresser And Various Tails
Department E
Ruins, Rooms & Reveries
Benebella *or* The Picture of Virtue

Not Long Now

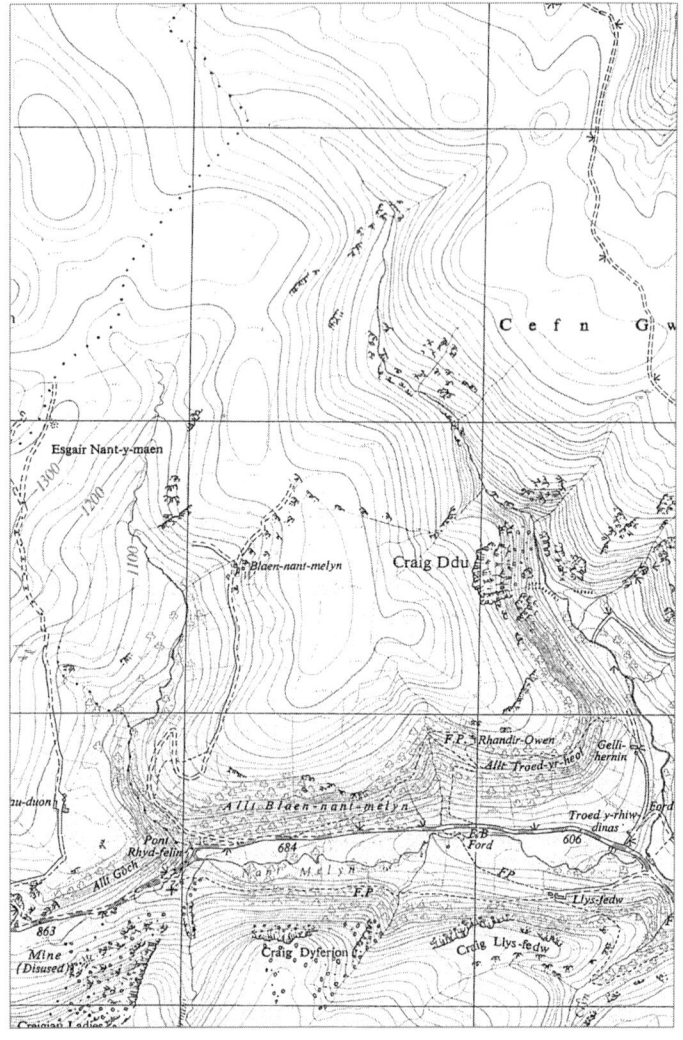

What wild winds moaning across the empty earth! What endless lashings of the pitiless rain! What mad rushes of sleet slung from nowhere, almost, against already-hoary brows, eyelashes ... and the mists, swirling ... And the darkness, and the endless tramping, climbing ... Who could have known it, who could have thought? That such a place existed, and so near to home? So near and yet so far, far beyond the thought of everyday things. So deep hidden in my longings, musings, for such a very long time ... and then, so very different, other ... from what I'd expected, imagined; and yet – had I known something of it once, before? I'd had this idea, long ago, of coming to this place. But it's not as though you just come, is it, just appear here, for the first time? A part of it has always been within you, ready for the place; and part of it has always been there, just waiting for you.

To be precise, accurate, I remember exactly when I first thought of it, this trip, this expedition (pretentious sounding? – well, not when you're here, doing it, as it were). I'd first got the idea when I was a painting student at the Slade art school, in London, or rather, when I first came to stay with Dewi Thomas. He was in the year above me, spent all his time in the pubs, as I recall, though he insisted he was always in the studio by eight – and after those nights, and all that beer! – youth! Dewi was from Llanybydder – well, I'd never heard of the place, obviously, until he took me, one vacation, to stay with his "Mam"; then, after a few more trips, I'd got to remember the name, and even – he had the patience of a saint – learned how to pronounce it. He'd said – idly, some time, perhaps while scraping his modelling clay, splashing brown water everywhere, or doing those crazy paintings of his – that the region just north-east of his place was the emptiest, bleakest area in the whole of Europe – less people, houses or farms; lots of sheep though. And I thought you must be mad, bit of a tall story, that – what about parts of Scotland? Then there was sure to be somewhere in Bulgaria or Latvia or somewhere, that was emptier; but they didn't stick in my thoughts, Latvia and those places, my imagination; Mynydd Mallaen, however, did. For a while I pored over maps (went to that shop in Long Acre where they sell maps of just about everywhere, all sizes and scales); it was, briefly, as though it called to me ... but then – you know how it is – I forgot it, exams got in the way, termly marks and assessments ... and the end of college loomed ... (I lost touch with Dewi, after a few years). But now, things are different ... at last ...

Our idea was to start at the northern end, work our way south. We spent the night in Lampeter, and I got a farmer to drive us up in a Land Rover, first to Llandewi Brefi, then east along a lane that got ever narrower, and finally petered out. Then, we were on our own, just the four of us (obviously, one man couldn't carry all that we needed, with the tents, the food, and everything else). We set out beside a forestry plantation, skirting the trees and steadily rising up the hill. Time and again I looked deep into the wood, beside the serried rows of pine trees, avenues like rich, dark caves, inviting us down into some other world. Next we struck out from the tree-side to climb the hills themselves. We had the idea, next, of working our way to the east, dropping down into the valley of a small river – Pysgotwr Fach, the map said – and following it around, towards the south. First the hill had to be negotiated, steeper than we'd thought, and probably the first real uphill hike we'd needed; there would be many more. Down the other side was a pleasant place, at first, with the river burbling across large stones, and smallish trees on either side. There was good weather, at that point, the sun shining down, but not too hot, and the trees and hills screening us such that we moved in and out of dappled light; we ate a little, there. At one point, we were walking in the bottom of a creek-like thing, rock-faces and steep rocky outcrops on either side. Our boots scraped against the small stones, and regularly we found ourselves walking in the water itself, which rushed over and about our feet, but didn't seriously drench us (wet feet, obviously, would not be a good idea; as the expedition was just beginning, I remembered to be always careful, on guard against any dangers I was tending towards, leading us into, through my inexperience). The river bed seemed to last for an age – winding and twisting, this way and that, but still, the compass showing me, taking us round in a great arc, southward and westward (so often, on maps, I have seen a road that seems to lead straight in one direction – but when you actually go along it, it is a series of small turns, to right and left). Regularly, it seemed, the river would be joined by another stream, from right, or left, so that the water was getting ever more and larger; and twisting around. Soon, the Tywi joined us, from the east.

My idea was never just to cross the land, in one direction, just to climb the mountain, and then head for our rest; the plan, always, was to double back, and head off in different directions, get to see a number of interesting places. Thus we followed the Tywi for longer than we might have done, intending to cross over the bridge to head towards Rhandirmwyn, though not wishing, till we had known the most desolate, to find habitations; that idea, at least, had always been uppermost to me – wildness was what it was all about, to seek out the very emptiness that could be found, get to really know it, become a part of it … not that that was really possible, no; it was so other, alien … too much so, at least, to then commune with it, become as one with it.

Not far from Rhandirmwyn – the river still swelling, but slowly – we turned and retraced our steps, stopping, first, to eat some more, but knowing that what we carried had to last. Walking now up the river, going in the opposite direction to before, meant that we were seeing it very differently. Well, as a painter I knew, immediately, that the light was very different, we were walking in the opposite direction, and the sun had moved around significantly. Before long, we had to strike out to our left – west – leave the river valley, and start to climb. This was much harder than we'd imagined, earlier, when we'd seen the flanking hill, though steep, as much more accessible than it actually was. I was glad of the food and tea, which we'd managed earlier; eating regularly, as normal, was good practice I knew, when it was possible – but the terrain would not always allow it. Nature, the place we were in, the land – I knew – was really in charge. We had only gone a few yards, and the land changed, changed significantly. In front of us – up above – the dour might of Mynydd Mallaen hovered, seeming to be lost in mist – and melancholy. It was decided that this was the place to make camp, to venture no further, not ascend the foothills at all – until the renewed light of next day showed our best route. I could tell that the mountain darkened the land, shut out the soft light that had made the river valleys so pleasant, cast its shadow all around, and perhaps – for the regions to its north – for a large part of the year.

Not Long Now

It was obvious, next day, that the weather was changing, and the congenial, temperate clime of the valley was in the past. Breakfast was a bit rushed, for I fancy there was a strong, silent, feeling that today, ahead, was a time of testing. Without words, all the gear was gathered together, the fire kicked away, and the day's tramping begun. The plan was to skirt around the north of the summit, by-pass it entirely, and go by way of Craig-y-Rhaiadr towards the west, into the very emptiest part of anywhere – nowhere, nothing, was noted on the map – heading for Pen-Cerrig-Diddos, and leaving the mountain itself for, perhaps, tomorrow, when the western regions had been explored, and the route turned eastwards again. Not an hour after breaking camp, the rain started, suddenly it came, not just falling hard, of course, but swept by the wind down the mountain's slopes. For the first time I pulled my visor down, and, of course, this restricted the view, separated and secreted one from the world outside. On and on in silence, trudging, always, with feet twisted up to one side, compensating for the steepness to the left, the ground falling away below. Hour after hour seemed to pass, and the wind howled more, and the rain crashed against me. Eventually – after a good part of the day had gone, it seemed – I stopped and took off my headgear (I could not get any wetter than I already was). The mist had come down hard, it was almost as though casting my visor off had had no effect, as though clear, unhindered, eyesight was no better, and gave no more vision, than before. Here I was, on a wild empty mountain, alone, surely ... and the mist swirling... But then – surely – no, a trick of the gloom, playing on tired eyes? Some kind of mirage that the mind had wrought from shadows that flitted in the emptiness? Surely it was ... a man ... a man all in darkness, walking towards me? No, it couldn't be! I replaced my headgear, and tramped on, kept my face to the ground, and covered a hundred yards or so – passed, surely, a half an hour, the windswept bracken tugging at tired legs, threatening, constantly, to trip me, send me crashing down the slopes – before looking out, again, at the gloom. Nothing. No – there he was again – coming towards me quickly, now ... I could almost see his face ... Walking quickly – despite the falling terrain, slopes too treacherous for any haste or carelessness – but never, *it seemed, arriving. Intent on me, hurrying, but always a little too far away ...*

I had to keep on, despite all, had further to go, yet ...Yet – I thought, consolingly – much had been done by me, much gone through, lived through, many places, and things I had done. Eventually – however long it was, however much more – a right destination awaited; eventually – welcoming, home – there would be Crowsavon ... not long, now ...

1

"Well, I don't know where he's been ... where he thinks he *is*, for that matter!" Hard, hard, hard! It was so hard, trying to do what was right, trying to do the best, to be fair ... to a father – well, father-in-law, in Rosemary's case – and one who'd not exactly played a big part in their lives, but who had always been, in his own way, *there* ... and a good man, really ... "I keep telling him, Crow's Haven's a really nice place, very clean and warm ... and the staff are really caring and professional ... *and I bet it's not like that in* all *these places* ... I *know* about these things."

"There's no need to lower your voice, no one will hear". Stuart was more pragmatic about things, knew that sleeping dogs were best left, felt sure that his father was basically happy, content, whatever that meant in his ... circumstances.

"And he says it's not Crow's Haven, like I keep calling it, but something ... well, proper Cornish ..."

"He's right. Well, we have been here a long time ... or him, at least. I've got more than a smattering myself. You know, I once had a real wish to learn it ..."

"Yes? Cornish?"

"Surely I've told you? That was before the lure of the bright lights – and college."

"Yes?"

"Well you know I'd gone through a big ... well, discovery of my roots thing – I suppose we'd call it today – when I was around, let's see ... early teen-age ... wanted to be all Celtic ... Not that they *were* my roots, really. Although I was born here, there was quite a bit of Birmingham in my past ... well, father's ..."

"I didn't know about that ... the Celtic thing. I mean, you're from St. Ives, yes, obviously I've always known that ... but weren't you keen to get out ...?

"That was later ... and the times ... Every rural kid was like that, from anywhere. Just think what it might've been like for a kid growing up in ... Herefordshire or somewhere, in the late '60s ... feeling like a country bumpkin whatever he did, wherever he went."

"Well, we didn't feel like that growing up in Basildon, I can tell you."

"No ...".

"Yesterday, when I brought the shopping in ... there was a bag, by the door ... packed. After a while, I realised what it was. I didn't like to ask about it ... and I didn't. But he volunteered. "How long?" – he said to me – "I'm ready" – and then something about "Home" – I said, Dad, you *are* home ... this *is* your home – you've been here for some time ... and it's a lovely place ... I've bought a nice warm dressing gown for you, for when the winter comes – I said"

"Yes ... maybe he'll use it, and maybe not. Yes, it's a nice place, but somehow, I find it a bit *functional*, don't you think?"

"Really?" He was always a building surveyor, wherever he went.

"Yes, clearly purpose-built. A lot better than when we first started coming here – the trees grown up nicely, masking it a bit".

"Really? Functional?"

"Before the trees filled out, you could get sight of St. Erth station, and that yard, and all the things around it ... houses, vehicles ... Yes, functional. I mean, it was clearly built as a retirement home, nursing home ... whatever it should be called. Many of these places are nice large Victorian houses, converted ... nice big rooms."

They fell silent, concentrating each on their jobs; Stuart going through piles of drawings (how they'd let him bring seemingly half his studio to the place, he didn't know), his wife sorting through the old man's clothes. What they were wondering about now, of course, was his future. Would they have to find some new arrangement for Dad (Rosemary tried to imagine Robert at home with them in Bromley, the Bohemian artist in London suburbia ...)? And all depended on Uncle Clive, who'd kept his cards – or rather, his will – pretty close to his chest; and Stella (yes, she really had been a widow in black, Rosemary thought, at the funeral) had revealed nothing at all (could you still easily get those black veil things? – well, presumably you could). Clive had always been a difficult one, but not the constant, undifferentiated coldness that characterised Stella ...(perhaps she'd found a shop supplying those Goths, say, in Penzance) and he'd immediately insisted on providing for his brother, coming down and finding the nursing home, personally looking over several. And paying. For all his ability to be unpredictable and boorish, he had no malice, it seemed, had never intended any slight to Stuart and her in not accepting any division of the expenses. Perhaps it was the publicity that had grieved him so much (*Local Artist Found Wandering In Carbis Bay, Midnight. Naked*), that made him act ... but how would Clive have seen that report? It hardly made the nationals. No, Clive had never played the much-more-successful brother, but it didn't take a professor of science – or whatever it was that he'd been – to work out that a struggling artist wasn't going to be in the same league. Actually, Robert had done reasonably well, but he'd never quite relinquished the role (Rosemary thought of that advert – cowboys expected always to prefer baked beans) that he'd long ago assumed. Well, in a couple of days, they'd know – just have to be patient, meanwhile; and Dad didn't look at all worried. He looked quite peaceful, actually. Some days he would be ... well, just normal for a very old man, talk a lot, about the past and suchlike ... Today ... it was as though he was off on his travels ...

2

Stuart had thought places like this didn't exist any more, except perhaps in books or period dramas; the old family solicitor's office – no, chambers – with yards of mahogany panelling, rows of leather-bound law reports, and a pin-striped gentleman solicitor with now-white remnants of almost curled hair, behind a large, ordered desk. The wooden filing cabinets seemed sure to contain no whiskey bottles, and the only computer had been on the desk – and pushed to one side – of Mr. Turley's secretary, in the outer office, who managed to convey old-world respectability while looking exceedingly smart, a hint of lacy ruffle at her collar, clothes that oozed quality along with restraint. You didn't find places like this where he spent his working days, in Croydon.

"Thank you … thank you for coming to see me … Do you know Truro? Yes – of course – born and bred down here, from what I recall …"

"Indeed".

"Right … er … the late Professor Levenham … concerning whom I've asked you to come …"

"Uncle Clive".

"Quite …I understand the funeral last …Thursday … was a dignified affair … family, but with representation from the university – London – and Mrs. Levenham, as they say, bearing up well… and his sons. Apparently a still young man, in today's terms … and so sudden – how tragic! …"

"Yes, quite".

"So, Professor Levenham's will … I have to point out that you are not directly named …"

"No, that's what I've always understood would … be the case. He was, of course, actually my father's half-brother …".

"So I understand, and much younger. But it's your father's … situation that I need to inform you of. You are aware that Professor Levenham organised, and provided for, his brother's care?"

"Yes, exactly, and would not accept any assistance from us. Generous to a fault, in this connection".

"Quite. Well, I have to tell you that his generosity is to live after him".

"Really?"

"Yes. Does that come as a surprise?"

"Well, a little ... but the arrangements ... Stella?"

"No, Mrs. Levenham is not ... involved. There is a trust, created by Professor Levenham, which he first consulted me about, soon after he came to live in Mevagissey ... er, that would be ... 1993 – seven, eight years ago – naturally, his solicitor was in London, before he retired, but the trust deed, etc., was not finally settled until last year. It will now come into operation, and provide the necessary resources till ... for as long as needed. Ah! Here's Lucy with our coffee!".

Calm order and quiet integrity would be the words – if he had searched for any – to describe the atmosphere of Turley & Drain, which Stuart almost consciously breathed in, as he stepped through the solicitor's outer office, knowing that he was unlikely to experience such a place again. Moments before he reached the door to the street, however, he was conscious of a different atmosphere, as a young woman entered, bringing, through the open door, the perfume of flowers that hung in baskets each side of the entrance. She looked at him, briefly, but seeing the secretary at her desk, moved forward, hesitantly, as though making enquiry without appointment. Then, Stuart was back in the pleasant Georgian street. For a moment, he had no idea where exactly he'd left his car.

3

"Who'd have thought!" – Rosemary had said this about three times, now. Neither of them had expected this outcome. Clive might well have willed some money, then left them to cope with any further expense after that, or take him to live with them (the question always before them – unsaid – was how long Dad would live). They'd begun to think of him as most likely coming to Bromley (Stuart had been unable to avoid a feeling of relief, when the thought of no more 600-mile journeys, which they regularly had to make, had come to his mind); better, though, to leave things as they were. Dad was sleeping again, and Stuart had, since yesterday, got to thinking that they wouldn't have to weed his papers after all, now, as the management at Crowsavon didn't seem to mind the amount of stuff he'd got (indeed, when he first came to the place, they'd suggested he bring his painting gear, and set up in a garden shed they had; he did, but then complained that its windows faced south, and were too poky; they offered an anglepoise lamp, but Robert had snorted ("What of the light! The Cornish light! The ripples on the water – the sky – why d'you think I came here in the first place?"). Stuart was looking out of the window lost in thought, considering the future, when, out of the corner of his eyes he saw a young woman (early 20s?) walk up the drive and disappear from the window's view, towards the entrance. "It's as well we share the driving", said Rosemary, seeming to read his thoughts. Then, *She looks familiar* – he thought, but at that moment Dad seemed to be stirring, waking, and he thought they might try, again, to tell him that though his brother had recently died, it wouldn't change anything for him.

A while afterwards – each wondering, to themselves, if he'd understood it, taken it in – there was a light tap at the door. Stuart went, and found one of the staff, who handed him a note. "Mr. Levenham ... someone just came to the door, asking if you were here – she wouldn't stop, just asked me to give you this."

Mr. Levenham – I need to talk with you – Could you make 6 tonight – by the Bed Pan (as I believe it's called)? If I don't see you there, I'll contact you again, and see if we can find another time that suits you better.

4

"I understand ... er ...that he was ... my father ...your uncle, that is ..." Stuart gulped, but tried not to look too shocked. "At least, my mother says so ..."

Barbara Hepworth's bronze sculpture *Epidaurus II,* installed in the Malakoff gardens, above Porthminster beach, soon became known as "the bedpan", at least to a few irreverent locals. Stuart had always thought of it as not a bad sort of addition for such a space; when much younger, he'd often asked to be held up to look through the hole, framing the bright sea, far beyond. Daisy Taylor was an arresting young woman – that's how she'd be described, he thought; tallish and rather willowy, laughter sparkling from her eyes, but with a strange, refreshing, seriousness – and this last comment, on top of what she'd so far said, seemed almost a logical conclusion. Stuart rose and wandered past the dwarf flower beds, intent on the outer wall and, once again, looked out at the shining water. Ms. Taylor – not that he would retain the *Ms.* for long – had indeed sought him out (and had visited Mr. Turley precisely in order to try to do so); or rather, sought his father.

"I asked if I could see him, Mr. Turley that is ... but not having an appointment, I thought, at best, he'd say come back next Wednesday, or something ... but some other client had had to cancel ... and then, when I stated my business, as it were, I thought he'd start talking about client confidentiality, and suchlike, and show me the door ... I expected some sharp young smoothy – you know the type – but he was an old sweety – don't you think? You met him."

"Weak before the charms of a ... young woman?" Perhaps "striking" was apt.

"Well, something like that. He actually ordered me a coffee from Miss Secretary. Then I gave him my spiel about being an art historian ..."

"Er ... like you've just ... to me?"

"Oh ... sorry ... but it's true – Hendon University; I teach Visual Culture modules – Why else would I want to meet you? That is ... your father. Mr – what was it? – Turley, explained about Robert Levenham's ... I'm so sorry ..."

"Dementia".

"Yes ... but he, Mr Turley, said that it might be possible to "direct scholarly enquiries", as he put it, to yourself, that he did know of Mr. Robert's whereabouts, indeed, had recently spoken to his son – well, a minute before, to be precise ... and I'd almost crashed into you."

"But ... your name did not cause any ..."

"Recognition ... no, I looked closely for that. I worked it into the conversation twice, just to be sure, but there wasn't a glimmer. He knew nothing of me. Neither, I assume did Mrs. Levenham."

"Stella? You contacted *her*?"

"Of course, I didn't breathe a word of ... what I'd been told. Just that I'd for some while been trying to learn more of Robert Levenham, and I'd read in the papers of her sad loss, and, did she feel able, at this difficult time – etc. – to give me a lead or two. Well, she just said – reasonably – that meeting would be out of the question, under the circumstances, but she would give me the address of Turley and Whotsit – she probably thought she was getting rid of me ... I thought if I try ringing them, first, they might get suspicious, and just refuse to see me, so, the direct approach ..."

"But what about ... the other thing?"

"Er ... Mr Levenham ..."

"Stuart".

"Stuart ... My father – the man I assumed was my father – walked out when I was twelve. Four years later, mother explained that he hadn't really been my father at all, sort of sixteenth-birthday present, but she didn't seem at that time to want to say any more."

"You were left ... in the dark ...?"

"Yes, exactly. Well, many years later – a week ago, to be precise – I did indeed come across an obituary, or rather, mother did ... quite shaken up, really ... and decided this was the time to tell me the truth."

"But you didn't announce this to Stella ... how did you find her?"

"The obituary said about him moving to Mevagissey, after retiring early from Imperial College, so it only took a few phone calls to get a contact address ... important local scientist dies suddenly ... facts about him were, as they say, "in the public domain". No, I only mentioned Robert, er, your father."

"So why did you ... tell me? And how, precisely, do you think I can help your ... studies?"

"Call it a woman's instinct but ... you don't appear to have been very close to your uncle ... *or* your aunt. I really am very interested in Robert's work ... but also in his life ..."

"No, I'm not. Life and work ... The two going together?"

"So often that's true ... And what I know already, what I seem to have found out quite quickly ..."

"And ... what is that exactly? And what about ... your mother and Clive ...?"

"I got the impression that I won't be told too much about that, by my mother ... yet ... but maybe in time. And there's my other source ...?"

"*Source?* I didn't realise there were such things as "investigative art historians!". What source would that be ... or are you like journalists? Keep such things to yourself?"

"No, my best source will be Grandpa Bernie, or rather, people who knew him ... Did you know of Bernie Lyme?"

"Er ... no, I don't think the name ..."

"Well, Bernie – my mother's father, died a few years ago – was an art dealer, became quite successful in the end. Not exactly Bond Street, but respected – Great Marlborough Street, actually. You definitely didn't know of him, from your father?"

"Er ... no, I'm sure ..."

"Well, he was always there, of course, but, looking back, I think Mum came to rely on her father rather more after dad went. So, there was always art about, as it were".

"Yes, the same for me, of course."

"Yes, I can imagine ... and artists ... Bernie knew a lot of people. The trendy, successful ones – not that many of them put any business his way – and lots of others ... Who I can now contact ... With Bernie's name ..."

"And, you're thinking, he may have known my father?"

"I can't be certain about that. Bernie probably knew *of* him ... but did he come to St. Ives much – or at all? I don't really know, yet. Do you think your father went back to London often ... after he settled here?"

"I don't think so, but he did go away from time to time, inevitably. You know, of course, that mother passed away – '83 – no possibility of help there ..."

"I'm sorry, no I didn't".

"So, what are your objectives now, I mean, what are you trying to do? See more of his work, or ...? I can show you where his studio was, where we lived, if that's any good ...?"

"Er ... yes, yes indeed ... Actually, I really hadn't got a plan – beyond trying to meet you, make contact ... Perhaps we could meet again, when I've made a list of questions – about his career and, as you say, works that can be seen ..."

Stuart got the feeling that the meeting – though it might be the first of several – was coming to a natural end. The sun had fallen, and, looking down to Porthminster, he saw that most of the bathers had gathered up their towels and gone.

" ... And, er, the ... other thing.", she said, cautiously.

"Oh, no, don't worry about that! I shan't be talking to Stella, or Mr. Turley, or anyone ... The nursing home ... Crowsavon – did you find it easily? ... they have some guest rooms for relatives, we'll be there for at least a further week ... Lelant ... very convenient. Here's a phone number that will reach us there."

"Thanks. I'll be in touch, then."

Daisy smiled, took the note he'd written, scribbled down her address, and walked off down towards the town. Stuart gazed after her – she was much younger, but was his cousin, if what she'd been told was right, if *she'd* told the truth. Then, he walked after her, down to where the buses stopped, above the Malakoff; he'd learnt, long ago, the futility of trying to take a car into St. Ives.

5

Daisy had not long eaten when there was a light, repeated tap on her door. Being past the end of the season, she'd managed to rent a holiday flat, for several weeks for a small outlay, part of one of the converted fisherman's cottages (or so she supposed it was) off the Digey, near Porthmeor. Who could this be? She carefully opened the door.

"Ah ... hullo ... I hope I'm not disturbing you ... Stuart – Stuart Levenham – has just told me about ... about your research ... May I come in?"

Bill Harvey was, Daisy thought, about Stuart's age, but more tanned, and casual. Apparently Stuart had thought to give him a ring, when he'd got back to the residential home (what was the place called? – Daisy tried to remember), and he'd explained to him about her interest in his father's work.

"Yes, Stu and I go back a long way – not that I've seen much of him in a while ... We both grew up here, but he went away, well, probably a good idea, as we both thought, at the time ... I didn't make it... Er, yes – I live just across the way – Stu said you were very interested, but – he thought – hadn't got much opportunity, so far, to see Mr Levenham's work – Robert, that is – and ..."

Bill – he insisted it was – behaved very nervously, but Daisy put it down simply to modern men being reluctant to get into a situation where they might appear as a threat to women, knowing that it could always seem, or be made to look, as though they were dangerous intruders; thus, she imagined, he acted as though guilty. In fact, Daisy didn't feel in the least insecure, and had no qualms about asking this stranger in, and talking about how, a while ago, she'd got very interested in Robert's kind of painting and eventually found herself here. (Actually, she realised – not even recording the care-home's name! – she hadn't been as methodical as she would normally, though the profusion of notes and books scattered around the flat certainly served to make her look as genuine as she was; it was actually Bill – she later realised – who was trusting *her* good faith). It seems Bill had developed a taste for his school-friend's father's work quite early on – or rather, he explained – his parents, initially. As a result he'd got twenty-six pictures on the wall at home and – to come straight to the point – would she like to come and see them some time?

"I'm sorry ... if that sounds, yunno, direct, *'Come upstairs and see my etchings!'* – that sort of thing" He gave a nervous laugh.

"No, of course ... No, that would be *really* helpful!"

"Er ... actually, there really are ... etchings, by Mr. Levenham ..." He said it almost sheepishly. "But he didn't do many" – this was added loudly, as though it was some kind of defence, exoneration.

"No, that would be very kind. Very good of you ... when might be ... convenient ...?"

6

Dear Daisy –

I do hope you didn't mind me phoning Bill Harvey. It was a bit off-the-cuff, but when I was on the bus, approaching Lelant village, I suddenly thought: Fool! Why didn't you suggest she contact Bill! He said he'd be going your way, later, and would look you up. Yes, he's got lots of Father's pictures. His parents took a few – well, thirty years ago, or more, sure to be – and then Bill did too (actually, at first I think they just felt sorry for Father, but Bill had a keen eye, from the beginning; might have been a painter himself). So I hope you're able to visit him, and see them.

Here are some facts I've gleaned from memory – all the forms we've had to fill in, in recent years (have you ever had Power of Attorney? I expect not):

Born: 1935, Birmingham.

Attended the Slade School of Art, University College London – I assume, early '50s.

Married: Mary Briggs, 1955. Mother came from Kent, and was a nurse in London (as is my wife) – St. Barts, I think.

Had a few trips to Cornwall in the mid/late-'50s (ie. before, and after, he was married) but didn't completely settle here till about '62 (I was born on an extended stay they had in Penzance – and my sister Rose – died only four). So, 1962 – he would have been 27.

Quite successful initially, but then (you'll know more about this than me, surely) his kind of work was very out of fashion – never been in, really – well not for seventy years or so!

Various things kept the wolf from the door. When I was at school (secondary,'70s) mother had a job in a shop in Fore Street; brought in a bit.

1982: Mother died; short illness. Father seems to have been very secure (materially, I mean) in the 1980s, though on his own. (I'd gone to be a student in the North, and then moved around for jobs – usual thing – so I don't have much day-to-day first-hand knowledge). However, it's now thought that he began, even then, to show signs of his later illness.

1992: One-man-show (I suppose we have to say "One Person Show" these days) put on at the Society of Artists here – only had to wait forty years! Yes, in a curious way he suddenly "made it" – or should I say made a come-back? – in his last years.

Mid '90s: Definitely not right, and deteriorating.

1998: First needed special care (his brother insisted on providing for this – went to Crowsavon, I think, in the following year).

I do hope these facts help – off the top of my head of course, so, probably not accurate. And I do hope you get to see some useful things at Bill's. His parents bought a picture showing the rocks at Clodgee, which I always thought was one of his best ever.

I hope to hear from you some time,

Stuart (Levenham)

7

"This isn't Crowsavon!", grumbled Robert, irritable at having been discovered, his intentions thwarted.

"Of course it's Crowshaven – where d'you think it is?"

Rosemary had found him actually on the point of leaving this time, well, leaving his rooms, his bulging bag on his shoulder; unpacking it – after finding it put out ready, that time before – had been futile. He must have waited till they'd gone up to their room for the night, and packed it again (the visitors' rooms were upstairs, the residents' on the ground floor; the visitors, it was assumed, would be able to climb the stairs, or operate the lift. As Stuart had said, the place was *designed* as a care-home; physical ability, or lack of it, had been planned for). She carefully manoeuvred him back into an armchair, said she'd make tea for them, they'd both enjoy that (Stuart had gone to Penzance to get a few things, and it *would* be just now, just when she was on her own with him, that Dad started getting wilful, fractious).

"I want to go … time to be going there … now …"

"But … Dad! Where do you want to go? Why? Why do you think this … isn't the right place – the place it's called … the sign, at the bottom of the drive … we'll go and have a look … if you like … nice walk – just a short one, though …:

"I tell you this is not … not it at all …"

"Well … but why ever … not …?"

"It's not! Look – Cornish … Yes? *Crows – avon*, or *Chy crows avon* – 'cross, or *across*, the river', 'House across the river' … or something like that. Welsh would be, er … *traws afon*. Is there a river anywhere here, eh?"

"Well …"

"No, exactly – nowhere near …"

"Well … that's as may be … but that doesn't change …"

"There! You see! It's just as I said!" But then, in an instant, from being agitated and fretful, he was wistful, sad. "Besides … it's not like it at all … well, a *bit* like it, but just … just …"

"What? What then…?", she asked. He seemed almost tearful.

"Just a … *shadow* …"

Rosemary wished that Stuart would come back soon, wished she'd said no, the things they'd needed could wait …

"…a shadow …"

8

There is none of Robert Levenham's work in the Tate St. Ives – this is as we should expect. From the beginning, he was an outsider, at odds with the times and the artistic ~~climate surrounding him~~ environment. The west of Cornwall was a revelation to him – its colours and climate, the quality of light – the very things that had drawn painters to Penwith for ~~about~~ a century or so ~~before~~. In particular – as is well known – in the late-1930s, and particularly after the Second World War, St. Ives was a virtual magnet for a new generation of British artists whose interpretation, and ever-changing re-interpretation, of their especial environment, ~~took the form~~ consisted – on almost all occasions – of abstractions of form that resonate subliminally with nature, and these very ~~ingredients~~ qualities. Levenham, however, could have traced his ancestry via such as Bratby and '50s "Kitchen Sink" realism, the Laura Knight of the gypsy pictures (late '30s), right back to London post-Impressionist movements such as the Camden Town group, before WWI, where, in particular, echoes of Harold Gilman can be found An authentic ~~survival product~~ recipient, and conduit, of British Neo-Realist traditions

Really, Daisy knew, she was not in the right mood to try to put her impressions on paper, to begin the task of writing a sensible, scholarly account of his work; she was too charged up, everything was too immediate; too recent. Reflection was necessary, sleeping on it, letting it gestate carefully, slowly; but she knew there was a virtue, also, in trying to produce something straight away, despite its crudity, despite all the changes that would be needed. The visit to Bill Harvey's house in Treverbyn Road had been a revelation. She had been wary, cautious, almost expecting disappointment (too chocolate-boxey, too touristey); his work could easily have been just that kind of thing, reacting so far from the abstractionists and avant gardists that it was just a slightly better-executed version of the things that sold in the harbour-side café she was sitting in right now. But it hadn't been like that at all.

What she had seen was a subtle and mature blending of many painterly traditions of the previous times brought together in a new way, drawing on the past but not *of* the past, yet standing out against the brittle novelty of so much that the critics lauded, even today, as the authentic "art of our time". And Bill Harvey himself had been – well, still edgy, unable to relax. Not many women in his life, she suspected, and here was one he hardly knew, let into what was obviously a very private world. The Rocks at Clodgee picture had indeed been memorable; where she'd feared a bright little landscape, ready for the wall of the better-class souvenir-buyer's home, she'd found a craggy, jagged composition, which seemed to rise some way beyond what might actually be found – even on this coast – to an almost lunar landscape, its depiction of reality teetering on the edge of abstraction. Other pictures had drawn on domestic interiors, with an almost obsessive clutter of everyday objects, suggesting more a junk-shop than a home. Surprising, though, was Bill's comment (she'd not thought like this at all, yet *she* was supposed to be the informed critic, the trained eye scouring the surface for its significance): "I think … well, it's just my idea … but … I sometimes think … *like* to think … that all these things, things in the paintings that is, have *meaning*, tell a story … But what?".

9

go HOme We KNow whO YoU arE and What Your ReaLly afteR

The message couldn't be clearer. It had been produced – rather old-fashioned, she thought – out of letters cut from a newspaper, pasted on a piece of lined paper (surely hate mail had moved on a bit? Wasn't it computer-produced, these days?). She could see straight away how they'd forced their way into the flat (a decrepit french window at the back, its frame now split). All her belongings were scattered, her books and notes torn, as though the intruders had had a frenzy. She'd only been out for an hour or so, just enough time to drink a coffee, and persuade herself that it really wasn't a good idea to start trying to write yet. She wondered just what kind of a sick ... she thought, then, to check the pile of clean underwear that she'd pushed into a drawer – you heard of such *things* – but it seemed unmolested. Whoever they were, they knew where to hit her; some things she might be able to stick back together, such as her papers; not the cover of *Artists in Newlyn and St. Ives, 1880-1930*, which had been torn off jaggedly. Soon the land-lady would have to be told (and the police?). Well, perhaps the message was right, perhaps she'd leave – done all she could here, for the present (Mr Levenham – Stuart – had been returning to London around now – tomorrow, or did he say yesterday?; of course she wanted to meet him again, but she could do that in London). Yes, she knew she'd be back (even Bill Harvey seemed to sense that); but later.

10

"All I'm saying is we have to be careful! The fact is we know nothing about her"

Just days after their return to Bromley, Rosemary had spoken to ... who was it? ... Angela from the reading group (or was it Sarah?), and she'd assured her – she'd worked in the education offices, for the council, where they'd had to liaise with higher education bodies – that there was no such place as the "University of Hendon", no, that had been an obvious lie. Stuart had told Rosemary all about his meeting with Daisy, and no doubt she thought he was easily taken in ("Well that solicitor certainly was – if what she'd told you was right – and rather forthcoming with the address! I think Stella was irresponsible ...").

"She struck me as ... totally genuine ... All she wanted to know about was Dad's work. I think he'd be rather touched by that, don't you?". Well, perhaps it *was* ... unnecessary to mention her, er, *paternity* business, to Rosemary.

"And what put her on to Dad in the first place?". Stuart realised he had no idea, hadn't asked.

11

"I regretted telling you straight away, almost". Rachel Taylor thought herself impulsive, *that* had been the cause of her action; but it was not to be undone, now. To be truthful, she'd thought about it several times before, knew her daughter's response would be philosophic, muted; but what with ... She wouldn't care to be questioned – the past was the past, and it wasn't as though there was Trevor around still (he would have reacted angrily to the fact that Daisy knew she, their only child, wasn't his).

"Mum, I don't want to know anything more – now let it rest". Of course she was curious about Clive Levenham FRS; but her mother would surely tell her more in time, *that* she was certain of (perhaps sometime when they were not in *her* house, like now ... places, settings, were important, she knew). Besides, there was going to be some sort of appreciation thing, profile, in the *Times Higher Education Supplement*, a sure source of information beyond the bare facts. *I suppose I should discover if there's any other legacy* – she thought – *the physical kind; well, his death was sudden, unexpected ...*

"Look, it really is his brother I'm finding out about – or trying to ... Now, the obvious lead is Grandpa Bernie – surely he knew artists concerned with St. Ives ... some other dealers, maybe – *somebody*? Can you suggest someone, somewhere where I might start?"

"Well I suppose there's Freddie Jackson ..."

"I've *heard* of him ..."

"Dad's partner, at one time ... if he's still alive."

12

At first, Daisy had been excited, but now was deflated. Indeed, if she admitted the fact, slightly depressed (back in her own flat, now, alone, at least she wouldn't have to confess to her mother, risk the inevitable "I warned you!"; pessimism, concerning the outcome, had followed Daisy's announced intention to pursue the lead). The ledger or account book, or whatever it was, had seemed to promise much, but just presented dozens of figures and entries which she either knew were of no use, or she could not interpret.

Meeting Freddie had been *very* interesting, no doubt about that. He'd suggested a café in St. Martin's Lane, after meeting at the entrance to the Portrait Gallery. She knew straight away which he was, and not because there were few people waiting there; no, Freddie stood out immediately. His age – Bernie's generation, for sure – but also his slightly Bohemian appearance, with scraggy beard and floppy hat. He even had a soiled velvet jacket; more at home, perhaps, in the Chelsea of 1970 – or 1890 – than the West End of 2001, or the slopes of Sydenham, where, apparently, he felt *very* at home, rarely venturing to town; "Those days are over", he explained, as he cast his twinkling eyes appreciatively over his young acquaintance, and stirred what seemed to her mountains of sugar into his cappuccino.

Clearly, there was too much pleasure, for him, in his meeting with this charming young person, to cause him to disappoint her by admitting – at least until absolutely necessary – that he knew nothing about this ... Levenshulme ... But he *did* have many memories of her grandfather – whom he'd only worked with in the later years of their careers, but nonetheless, he had actually known for a long time. Indeed, he was quite sure she, Daisy, had visited the shop – but that was in a push-chair, on one of the few times Rachel had looked in on her father, at work; he didn't immediately share that particular memory with her, considering, perhaps exaggeratedly, the extent to which young people do not relish being reminded of their toddlerhood, and marvelling again and again at what a supremely comely young adult she had blossomed into.

The business of being an art dealer, in those years, had really been quite splendid. First, the heady atmosphere of the Swinging

Sixties – he wished he'd been with Bernie then, just a few yards from Carnaby Street, of course – and even the dismal years just after had not been without their zest. But it was the '80s, of course, that had been such a good time for them – things on the up, plenty of money around – even if it was in the hands of slippery young rogues in suits – and that was when they felt they'd arrived; "Go out on a high, Daisy, go out on a high!" (they'd sold the business, apparently, in '91 or '92 – Freddie wasn't sure; Daisy vaguely knew of this, remembered; she'd been at school at the time). He banged his wrist, in emphasis, against a ragged envelope on the table, which contained a thickish book. He'd found it after rifling through some of the crumbling boxes he permanently kept, apparently, on the stairs, the cause – along with several piles of books there, and his cat – of at least two cleaners resigning in protest at their safety risk to themselves ("Absurd! I've never tripped on anything! Well rid of them, I say!"); now, the dust just fell softly, and settled undisturbed.

"I don't know if it'll help. It's just a record of things we sold, and who produced them. I'm not sure what years it covers – not all, certainly, but, despite searching, I couldn't find any more like that."

"Thank you, that's *so* kind … but …"

"Yes?"

"How shall I return it?"

"Oh, er … well, yes, er, I *would* appreciate it back … Best not to post it though … best not to risk …"

It *was* from the 1980s, the good years, and it did, indeed, record picture titles, artists' names, exhibition dates, and one-man-shows and the like; and money (she saw several names she knew, whose owners, now, would be embarrassed to have it revealed how little they were selling for, then). A great many, of course, meant nothing to her, people, probably, whose early success had faded (she noted that these people had been selling, at that time, for no lesser figures than those who'd later become well established – but had moved on, surely, from Bernie and

Freddie). After a while, one name did stand out. For one thing, it came up time and time again as the decade proceeded, and for another, the artist commanded *very* high prices. It was no surprise that this Daniel Titus was another name that she knew nothing of; but none of the obscure people had made *this* sort of money. But there was no Robert Levenham, not a mention.

13

She just had to look harder – Daisy sighed, determinedly – had to pursue another angle, think of something else; something to do with Levenham, that was – because the biggest downside of finding no leads in the ledger was that it loosed her mind to dwell on the *other* thing, that which she'd hoped to forget: who it was, and why, that'd trashed her flat in St. Ives? Whoever it was, they seemed very nasty – the note revealed clear premeditation – and no doubt capable of worse things. She felt sure she'd be safe here, with however many miles it was between herself and Cornwall; but *who* and *why* remained, and undoubtedly she would, eventually, want to return. She could only think that it was something to do with her discovery that she was Clive's child; what a fool she had been, telling Stuart! He must have told someone (she couldn't believe it was him, why else would he have continued to help her, tell Bill Harvey about her work? But maybe she'd been taken in by him, somehow, lulled into false security ... *I'm so impulsive, sometimes* – she thought). She'd hid the note, and managed to convince the police that it had just been a random break-in; the land-lady seemed reluctant to make any more of it than she had to, realising, no doubt, that the defective french window had been her fault, and a lot of investigation would reveal the extent of her responsibility. At least – Daisy now considered – it had been wise to keep it to herself, just quietly pack and get the next train, not go to the care-home and make a scene .... But she had also wondered about the solicitor ... perhaps he'd just *seemed* not to realise who she was? No, this was crazy ... solicitors don't organise break-ins (the thought of – *what was he called?* – cutting letters out of old newspapers, while his cocoa cooled, brought a much-needed smile to her face; tweedy dressing gown and slippers, she supposed). Telling no one back home had been the best choice, as well; her mother really would regret her revelation if she'd heard about the intruders.

14

Daisy was amazed, and couldn't hide it.

"You must remember that in 1967 it was only a few thousand ..." But what a house! "And Jean – my first wife – was a barrister's daughter ... Yes, I'm an absolute expert on marriage, much experience – married four times. Though, Jean died ... others would have got their hands on part of this, otherwise, sure to have done ..."

Freddie was the second man Daisy had met in a month who was delighting in showing her his possessions, his home; only Freddie had a few more of them than Bill Harvey. She knew that he had nothing there concerned with Robert Levenham, pictures, documents or memories, and he could give her no leads, nothing to take her further; and at first she'd thought the longish trip, changing at Clapham Junction, and the uphill trek from Crystal Palace station was more like something she *had* to do, than the source of wonder it became.

"The basement's separated off now – *Darren – he's "in futures" – whatever they are*" – he whispered – "that's his BMW outside. Helps pay the rates – the Council Tax I should say – that's the biggest thing, now ...".

And there they were – Chinese vases, Art Nouveau figurines, Sixties memorabilia in frames, and Freddie's special joy, his collection of Bernard Leach pottery.

"I suppose that's my one and only connection with Cornwall, actually ... never thought of that, but ... Again, they were very cheap when I was young."

But there was no evading Daisy's disappointment, and her real objective; he gratefully took the ledger from her hands, but made light of it, and promptly offered tea – "Or would you prefer something stronger …?"

Freddie bustled off to the kitchen, something stronger having been declined, and, indeed, it was too early, for him at least, he claimed. Daisy looked around the large room. She recognised the Leach pots, though there weren't actually that many of them. Returning, he seemed to have read her thoughts.

"Of course, lots of things had to go … Angela, you know … third wife … needed her pound of flesh." But there was quite a lot remaining.

"Well, I could find no reference to Levenham, no mention at all", she said. It had to come some time. "But … I noticed a few names that are now big. I can see things were going well, at that time."

"Yes, indeed, mustn't grumble". *I'll say not!* – thought Daisy. "I kept noticing this … Titus was it? Seemed to command quite a figure – where is he now?"

"Really? Oh, Daniel Titus, yes … yes, we did very well on his behalf … sold several to the Saatchis – three, I think … and then, following their lead, there were quite a few other City people".

"I don't think I know his work".

"No … sort-of 'Neo-Surrealist', I suppose you'd say – though excuse my amateurish labelling … can't think that phrase would go down well with proper critics and … such as yourself … No, not really me – too weird – but with the public it was a storm … er, that part of the public who could pay for it, obviously … then, just as quickly gone … I think there's one in the Tate Modern … but I shan't be going there to look at it … No, I'm sorry you've drawn a blank, here, with Levenham … what a shame …" – and they both realised he felt as disappointed as she did; and his mind was clearly elsewhere:

"Can I say, you're *just* the image of my grand-daughter, Rebecca … well, as she was when she moved to Australia." He wore a distant look, but then returned to the subject of art: "I had several, once ... Titus's ... Angela liked them ... her sort of thing – *she* had money ... took them with her." Then a ginger cat scurried into the room, and lo and behold, he seemed to take to the young woman, and she to him. "Actually, there's still one here, somewhere ... Titus, I mean ... can't think where ... He's called Bacon *Aren't you?* ... – that's after the stripes, I should say, not that nasty painter ... sometimes I call him Streaky, sometimes Back ... I keep threatening to sell him to Sainsbury's, I know *they* can shift a few rashers, make light work of him ..."

"Erm ... Could I ... where ...?", asked Daisy. It took Freddie a moment's realisation. "Oh ... I'm sorry, my dear ... yes, er ... across the hall, first right".

Even the cloakroom was big. Daisy shut the door behind her, slipped off her trousers, and sat on the loo. Eventually, she looked up and around, her eyes finally fixing on a far wall to the right of the doorway. There, half covered by an old anorak, was the oddest painting she'd seen, crudely fixed to the wall. It seemed to be a landscape, but the tops of the hills were sprouting either vegetation or flames, and a river seemed to have great waves running *up* it, as though an estuary in full flood-tide. Meanwhile, unconnected, there floated, across the picture-space, a collection of ordinary domestic items – tin-opener, teapot, whisk – and in the left corner there was what resembled a pile of rotten offal (perhaps Francis Bacon had a place in Freddie's house after all). When she'd finished, she walked closer, moved the anorak away, and took a hard look. Yes, it was Titus, alright, as a bold signature confirmed (each letter was painted in a different colour ... pretentious, she might have called that, if the whole thing hadn't been so strange). Perhaps Freddie never used this cloakroom.

"I think I've found your Daniel Titus for you!", she announced, returning to the living room. Freddie was wrapped up in the pleasures of tickling his cat's tummy; Bacon wore a look of grim endurance.

Odd, very odd – thought Daisy – *and yet* ... At dingy, dirty Balham station, a dainty, thin woman in ornate Japanese costume carefully stepped into the train, followed by a suited Japanese man; they looked beautiful, both of them, like delicate flowers growing in a rubbish dump. You saw the strangest things in South London.

15

What great cavernous spaces! Tall, thin steel legs that bubbled with rivet-heads, rising up into the bright emptiness. Daisy never failed to marvel, to stare upwards, to look more at the place itself than the things in it. Naturally, she'd been to the gallery many times, knew almost all that was to be seen ... and all art galleries had something of their own, some special magic; but when it came to *space*, the Tate Modern surely had it, and, of course, that was because of what the building had been, a power station – and she thought of it, not filled with sight-seers and culture vultures, but as the generating station that not long ago it was, humming with machinery, great whirring engines of power whose buzzing and crackling – or whatever they did – surely filled the space. Now all she had to do was find this painting. She felt a bit odd having gone off at a tangent. She'd made phone-call after phone-call about Levenham, enquired with absolutely all the galleries and museums, the Slade and the other London art schools. Nothing. And for the first time, she began to wonder if that particular topic – the work of Robert Levenham – was really going to be the thing for her; and so she had allowed herself to become more and more curious about this Titus bloke ... well, if this place had acquired some of his work, they'd have to have known something about the man; and no one else seemed to know about Levenham, except herself, and his family, and ... the man in St. Ives ... And if she herself had not known about Daniel Titus, at least he seemed to have a place in the art establishment's consciousness – at least in the past – which was more than Levenham did.

Up and up staircases she went, along the floors of thin oak boards, past Hockneys and Rothkos, past that pasty-looking girl in her sick-yellow wrap who wistfully exposed a pallid breast while clutching the other; past agonised Picassos and spindly Giacommettis. Soon it would be another academic year, and droves of students would be making visits, and sitting through classes looking at slides of just these paintings, visits and classes which she normally took – but not next term … but the Titus that Freddie said they had, that *would* be something new for her…

Room after room, spaces light and shaded, white, light rooms revealing all the City through strip windows … but no sign of anything like she'd seen in Freddie's cloakroom. In the end, she turned and descended, found an information point and asked. At first, the woman leafed through a battered glossy booklet, then searched in a drawer for a typed list; in concentration, she pushed a clutch of ginger hairs back behind her ear, as though their wilfulness, alone, frustrated her determined searching. But then her demeanour changed, and she turned on Daisy a little of the expression reserved, perhaps, for those whose enquiries made no sense, people who maybe thought to find their own particular favourites within this awesome space … "Daniel … who was it? No, I'm sorry …" Whatever had made her think Freddie would have been right? Maybe he'd meant some other gallery?

16

Totally deflated; that's how Daisy felt for certain, as she returned back home to her flat, tramped up the stairs, got her key out feeling tired, leaden. So it came as quite a surprise – a nice one – when, checking her phone messages, she heard an unfamiliar voice:

" …Er … Ms. Taylor? … er, Darren Scott here – Freddie's tenant? Freddie Jackson? Freddie gave me your number, said you wouldn't mind me calling? Apparently you were interested in Daniel Titus? We have one

at the office – Perhaps you'd like to drop in some ... see it? Well, the offer's there ... give me a ring ..."

Well – how about that! Darren was obviously one of the many people, these days, whose voice went up at the end of each sentence. Well, if the Tate Modern couldn't provide sight of any of this artist's work, she'd certainly try Darren. Futures indeed ...!

17

"Apparently the firm bought this in '89 – what's that? – twelve years ago now; before my time, obviously. Apparently Gerald Goddard, one of the founding partners, thought it symbolised the fruits of the free market, the future, where things were going? *Do you think it – aged a bit?"* – he whispered – *"I do".*

The offices of GLGN were just what Daisy had imagined a large, international finance house in the City was like; just as she'd anticipated, despite never having been in one in her life (why *was* that, she wondered, why were they so predictable?). Near the Barbican, north of the Museum of London and the Guildhall, there it stood with several others, with its acres of reflective glass, a glistening bronze tower that surely shot up higher than the one at Babel ever had, and inside, there were competing acres of travertine lining the walls and floors – and even the ceiling, in places, where it was not clad with mirror-glass. Darren had explained; "GLGN – that's Goddard-Levin-Gieves-Neustein – I think just remembering all that was given as a test of competence, in the interview" He paused, as though for a laugh, but when his audience just smiled thinly and nodded, he proceeded. "Well, anyway, it seems Goddard was going to Liberty's one day, and saw it at ... er, Freddie's place – and your grandfather, wasn't it? Thought it was just what we needed?"

Daisy hadn't thought Bernie had ever had a window large enough to show such a work, but she must have been mistaken. The centre of the work was a flower, a large sunflower-like plant that grew out of a glass bowl that had just clear water in it. The flower had no roots to support its massive growth, and, inevitably, such a plant would have needed a far more hefty pot than this little dish. There were several flowers, actually, and each one seemed rather different, with aeroplanes and limousines, of all things, coming out of one, and another issuing crowds of people all dressed strangely, like they were at a pop festival. Down in the lower part of the picture – as with Freddie's – there were all kinds of domestic implements, but each one painted in violent colours; and there were men dressed in suits seeming to be riding the Tube – well, this was the '80s – no doubt on their way to Bank.

"It's actually supposed to be called *The Fated Flower* – sounds rather gloomy, doesn't it? But that's not what it meant to Goddard, I think, nothing gloomy, I mean, or pessimistic?

"So ... you live in Freddie's basement-flat?" Daisy, for the minute, didn't want to discuss art with this voluble young financier; and she did not, for one moment, take her eyes off the work.

"Indeed. I say, 'Not so much a *pied á terre* as a *pied sous terre*', yes?" Again he seemed to pause, for at least a smile; but Daisy was unobliging. No, Darren was quite dishy in his way, sure enough, but – just as she'd thought that day in Freddie Jackson's cloakroom – she strangely felt that there was more to this work than initially met the eye; and that meant more than she, at least, normally saw in this kind of painting.

"So, did this Mr. ... Goddard buy any more of Titus's work? ... Any others for your offices?"

"No, I don't think so. He's not ... around any more ... That is, not in any sense ...?"

"Oh!", said Daisy. What strange ways, today, people had of referring to death. "And Titus? Freddie seemed to know *nothing* about him?"

"Oh, I think he remembered a little ... later ... something about him – Titus, that is – disappearing into some remote place ... Wales I think? ... Or maybe that's where he always was ... not sure."

"So *he's* ... not 'around any more'?"

"No – as Freddie seemed to think …"

Daisy ascended the glass spiral stair that dizzily coiled its way up into an atrium whose open space, between office floors, narrowed, then opened out again. She could see the large painting better that way, from half-way up its length. At the bottom was the multi-coloured signature she'd expected (its letters each ten or twelve centimetres high). But above, near the glass bowl, she felt sure she'd seen something else … a trick of the light? Higher, nearer, the light would be different, she felt sure. She strained forward. There it was … but it was not anything painted, no different colours, or texture … just light, a different reflection … something not easily seen (well, perhaps never seen – even if you were looking). It was as though a garden snail had slithered across it, left its trail … but this was not just a straight path or patterns of meandering, but letters … definite meaning … Of course! It was simple artist's picture varnish! This was a kind of clear glazing material that most artists, until recent times, had used to embellish their work, bring out the highlights, and cause even darkness, the shadows, to look lustrous. This artist had applied it, not just with a large flat brush, coating the surface, but with a narrow paint brush – say, No. 10 – … She held her right arm out, shielding this part of the picture from incoming light. *YDRAL … HYD … LYS …* something like that. Darren realised she was onto something.

"Er … is that … something … you've seen? Of interest …?" Daisy returned to the main floor, to the waiting Darren, who seemed pleased as punch that she'd obviously found it worth coming to see.

"Darren, this has been *very* interesting, thank you!" But she didn't go into details, or tell him more.

"Oh … well … I'm so glad. *So* glad …" For once, his voice didn't rise at the end of the sentence. He walked with her to Moorgate, fascinated, apparently, to learn about life in one of the … new universities. "I *do* hope we can meet again?"

This time, she did not arrive back at her flat deflated; but again, there was a phone message requesting a meeting; *and* – she thought – *perhaps it's best to go …*

18

"I'm so glad you were able to come ... would have been a pity to have missed this opportunity to meet up again ... see how you're doing".

The hotel – one of those in Bloomsbury, not far south of Euston – had obviously been a large private house, originally, but not for a long time, Stuart thought. Really, this was *not* his kind of thing, not the way he'd prefer to be spending the day; so an opportunity to meet with Daisy, in the lunch break, was very welcome. They had to do this every year, go on a management training day; it was all part of Council policy, now. In the office, the department called it the Away-Day, dreaming of Brighton. At least it was out of the Borough, with travelling expenses and a good lunch provided; but four hours of presentations, break-out groups and plenary meetings, devoted to such riveting subjects as health and safety in the work-place and embedding the law's equal opportunity requirements in departmental policy statements, was not the way most of his crowd wanted to spend their time. The others, after eating, had headed for the Tottenham Court Road shops, but he had hovered in the hotel entrance, until he saw a slightly-flustered young woman rapidly head his way, craning her neck upwards at sign after sign, on the different hotels and offices. "I'm so sorry – broken rail at ... Camden Town? Canning Town? – something ... Have you been waiting long?"

"Not at all. Shall I order coffee for us ...?" The hotel had a pleasant lounge, just the right place for them to sit and talk. She took off a light jacket and a waitress arrived with a tray. Immediately, he sensed that things were not right; a certain coolness in her manner.

"So – how are things? Your work going well?"

"Yes ... well, no actually ... I can't seem to discover *anything* about Robert Levenham."

"Oh dear ... I mean, is there a way I can help?"

"Maybe, maybe not ... Er ..."

"I hope ..."

"No ...er ..."

"No, you go first ..." Stuart felt sure, now, that something was wrong. How different from that time in the Pedn Olva gardens!

"It just that ..."

"Yes?"

"It's ... I had a ... distressing thing happen, the day before I left St. Ives ..."

"*Yes?*"

"Well, that was the reason I ... decided to leave when I did".

"Tell me".

"On that afternoon my holiday flat was broken into".

"No!"

"Yes, my things were all gone through, so it appeared, some books damaged."

"No!"

"Well, the police thought it was just a routine crime against tourists, you know, people on holiday who don't take the precautions they would at home ... But there was more to it than that. I didn't tell them – or the landlady – but the first thing I found when I got there was a sort of note. You know, the old business of letters cut out of newspapers ... '*We know what you're really after*' I can only presume they meant something to do with my ... the paternity thing ... Must have thought I was after inheritance or something, establish my rights, identity ... isn't 'gold-digger' the phrase?"

"No! But ... how can that ..."

"That's what I wondered, and I'm afraid ... I could only conclude ... I have to ask ..."

"I told no one, *no* one ..."

"It was my fault, I shouldn't have just told a complete stranger ..."

"Daisy, I told no one ... not even Rosemary".

"No? Not your wife?"

"No. No one."

"Well how else could anyone have found out? Or what other motive could they have had? What else could anyone have thought I was doing ...?"

Stuart was worried now. How otherwise could it look? It was natural that she'd been suspicious of him. "Daisy, honestly, I told no one about that, neither Rosemary, nor Bill Harvey nor ..."

"What about Professor Levenham's family?"

"I've not communicated with them at all, not since the funeral ...and then we left as soon as we respectably could."

"And Rosemary?"

"I'm sure she hasn't ... besides, what would she tell them? A young woman from a university wanting to study father's work? But you told Stella that yourself ..."

"Yes. So I did. Well, it's a mystery then ... but I don't feel like letting them deter me, whoever 'they' are". She was calmer now, he thought, and satisfied by his assurances – well, she should be ... what possible purpose could *he* have had ...? No wonder she had seemed tense, at first, icy ... then Stuart realised that his own words had raised something that Rosemary had set him wondering about ... perhaps now was the time to ask.

"Er, I said about the university ... you do research into things, as well as the teaching you mentioned? So where was it ... north London somewhere ...?"

"Yes, Hendon. We're called 'The London University of Hendon' now ... used to be 'North Western' until recently ... once used to be a polytechnic ... People thought we must be in Lancashire or somewhere ... it was decided that you had to put 'London' in the name ..." She'd anticipated his query ... so this was why Rosemary's friend had never heard of 'University of Hendon' "Yes, 'LUH' we all call it. Apparently, if you're after overseas students – as we all are – they all know where London is ... up the road from Heathrow ... it matters."

"Oh, so that's why I'd not heard ..." He thought it best not to say more, or she might get to think he'd wanted to check her out ... Fortunately, she changed the subject herself.

"No. I'm afraid I just can't find anything at this end. Actually ... I think I might return to Cornwall soon; I'm not going to be put off. I've been given a sabbatical to do this – no teaching or anything, next term ...but only one term." No, Stuart could see she wasn't the sort to be easily deterred.

"Well that's interesting because, when we were going through Dad's things, we came across some papers that – looking back – I didn't think of it at the time – might contain something useful to you. I'll have to go down again myself, before long, and I'll have another look, see what I can find ..." It had been wrong of them, he realised, to doubt her. He really must look at the pile of stuff at Crowsavon; there was *sure* to be something there. Then, depressingly, he suddenly realised that the afternoon's programme was minutes from beginning; time to return to the clutches of policy goals and strategic implementation ... He must have indicated, by his sudden stiffening and anxious looks over her shoulder towards the conference room, that their time was over.

"Oh ... just one thing before ... Have you heard of someone, a painter, called Daniel Titus?"

"No. Can't say I have".

Later, towards the end of the sixth dreary presentation of the day, he realised that he hadn't asked her what he'd meant to ... what had first alerted her to Dad ...

Not Long Now

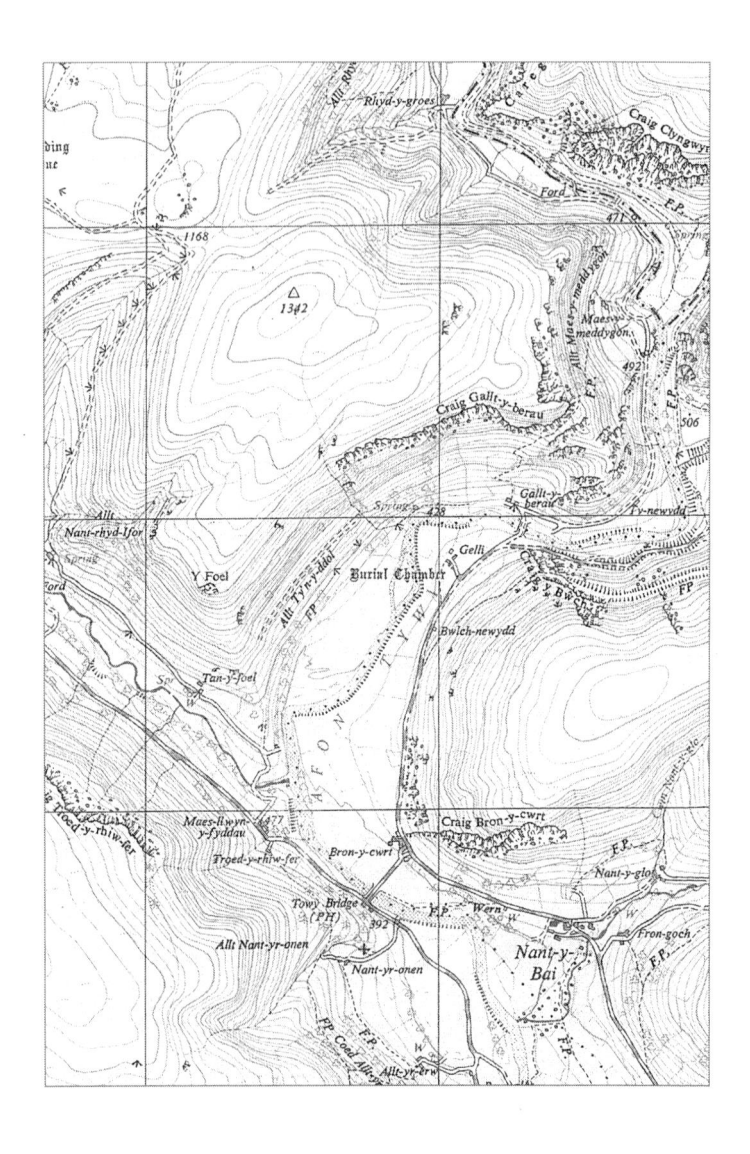

It proved to be much harder than I thought. Turning east again, setting our faces to the mountain itself, Mynydd Mallaen ... – I could see it plainly at times; at others, it seemed to hide behind small ridges and bluffs, as when bushes and small trees seemed to block out our view entirely. And there was the mist. It was as though the mountain was shy, coyly hiding its face from me, but peeping out at times, intent on revealing, just in parts, how awesome it could be, how difficult; as though it was unforgiving, remorseless, knew its power over me, its tendency to harshness. Yet, perhaps, here was a kind of mercy, in that it held from me the full extent of its ability to weary me, wear me down; it gave me a kind of come-on – intense, irresistible – while hiding its fullest ability to cause despair. The mist fell sudden – as I had thought it would – but also came with a kind of powdery, golden-brownness when – as happened, from time to time – the light shone onto it. I can only call it 'light', a soft glow; it was not the sun, the full bright disc, which didn't exist anywhere – so it seemed – in the world as it was here, in this place.

Now, my legs seemed to be buckling, my knees crumpling and folding as I climbed ever upwards, my bent back reaching forward, as it were, to scale the heights, to press onwards, upwards. The thick clumps of earth, terraced by the sheeps' tracks, were every time the objectives, the things I scaled, and strove up on. Or it was swathes of loose scree, stones just the wrong size – too large to crunch over, too small to just clamber between – so that every object before and beneath me had to be negotiated carefully around, my eyes, my face, always down upon; so often I must needs look to that below, before me – lost in the small, the commonplace – never to the far horizon, the summit; the objective. But at least it was not raining (times were when I was as damp inside my clothes, with sweat, as ever the rain soaked me outside); but at least there was no lashing into my face, and so my eyes could be uncovered much of the time (the tight cramping of goggles, strapped around my head had, on occasion, been maddening, causing a choice of miseries, either the tightness of the straps, or the rain-lash).

Often when we were minded to pause (and I acceded to that) I looked at the sky, and tried to read the changing clouds, which, in a wind-driven moment transformed themselves from lazy herring-bone to a harsh, angry darkness, threatening the worst of all weathers (the most typical). And the nearer the rain seemed to get, the more I warmed, comforted myself with thoughts of that soft warm bed that awaited, at Crowsavon; and it was when I did so that I heard – not saw, this time, heard – the voice of the Man hailing me, the strong, but gentle, voice of the Man, calling.

19

"There's quite a hefty bolt on the shower door, and I really *don't* have the rotten carcase of my mother in the cellar!"

Daisy gasped. "No, I'm sure! No, look I'm really very grateful … entirely happy with the idea. There's really no need to give such … assurances …"

She had bumped into Bill Harvey quite by chance, by St. Eia's, heading towards Fore Street. Coming to see him had been a prime objective in returning to St. Ives, seeing his pictures once again; but she'd thought to choose her time to knock on his door, after a day or two finding somewhere appropriate to live. She'd left London without making any prior arrangements, and checked in to an inexpensive hotel for a few nights; but now Bill was offering the use of his spare room, that she stay there for as long as she needed. He said he was out a lot, and she'd have to "do for herself" (presumably, that meant getting meals etc.); clearly he was uncertain as to if it was alright with her, this offer, hence his joky reference to *Psycho*; but a forty-ish man living alone in his parents' house was hardly weird, these days, what with the cost of buying one's own, and the fact of single living being more common now (but yes, it had been a slight surprise when, the last time they'd met, Stuart had told her that Bill had a daughter living in Redruth).

"Actually, we don't have a cellar, and the parents were cremated. Yes, we used the spare room quite a bit once, but then Dad increasingly had it as a kind of study, place to put papers and things – this means that you'll have a desk to work at, spread out a bit. How about coming round tomorrow evening? I'll make up the bed".

20

This time, she was able to look in greater detail at each picture, above all, looking alone, moving slowly from one to another and next another, and then, finally, back to the first; this time, she was not quite so much of a visitor who had to be polite to a hovering host, make the right noises while they looked on (earlier that day, Bill had said something about having to go to Penzance). Bill's father had been something in the local authority, and one who, apparently, had increasingly brought work home, hence the large desk, which now she used for her notes and books. Bill saw the damaged state of one of the books, and that had given her an opportunity to raise the one matter that she felt she would have to raise: the break-in. She'd decided to give Bill the edited version, which just suggested a random crime with associated vandalism, not mentioning the accompanying note – the inference of premeditation – or the possible cause; she said nothing about the fact of Robert Levenham's brother having turned out to be her natural father. Bill just thinking of her as an art historian studying Robert's work – with no possible connection to the family, or source of any other concern – was best. The least complications, the less muddy the water, the better (she told him at length how, in all universities these days, academic staff were urged to do research and publish papers, the results of which had to be collated, and figures produced for the government inspectorate). He'd been distressed to learn about the break-in, of course, and she'd looked at him closely when recounting it; it was not *totally* impossible that he was involved, she knew, but she doubted it, and the look of surprise in his eyes (genuine, she thought) had convinced her that she'd assessed the position correctly (still, was it not *mad* – a small voice asked – going to live in the house of a ... remote possibility? No, she assured herself, trust to judgement, just this once; the advantages, here, were many ...). And then, after telling him about the break in, she'd changed the subject: Had *he* heard of artist Daniel Titus? – she asked; Stuart, she said, had not.

"No ... er ... who's he?"

"Oh, he was just a painter that ..." – and what followed was a whole explanation about Grandpa Bernie, Freddie Jackson, and even Darren Scott and GLGN. Bill seemed to find much of this interesting – or rather, found her research, and the places it had taken her to, very interesting; but concerning "Daniel Titus", he said, his mind was just blank. But looking carefully at the paintings, today, Daisy became convinced: there was some sort of connection between Titus and Levenham.

In several of the oils before her, she noticed a small glass bowl filled with clear water – different from Titus's, of course, but ... it was as though they had some link, some common ... roots of some kind, which they had shared ... Ridiculous, of course, an idea built on a bowl of water! ... No, it was instinct, she realised, intuition ... But – with the mental equivalent of a crashing, banging sound – a voice in her head told her that it was *scholarship* she was involved in – *evidence* was what she needed, was all that counted (how thin, now, seemed those old accounts of historic art, which merely stated, quite without foundation, the roots and connections of things, certainties based simply on the supposedly-great-scholar's whims ...).

21

Soft, faded pink – delicate and fragile, now – *The Language of Flowers* was a lovely little Victorian book, the sort that a coy young man had given to his betrothed, or the gentle, delicate young lady that he hoped he might one day call his betrothed. Indeed, the book that Bill showed Daisy had a suitable original inscription in it: *"To E – with all my love. J."* – it seemed almost obtrusive just to read it. But in recent times, apparently, it had belonged to Robert, though Bill knew of no romantic occurrence by which he might have acquired it; "Found it in a second-hand shop, more like – plenty around ... Truro perhaps ...". The book contained a list of flowers and plants, in alphabetical order, and next to them, the equivalent meaning: "Acacia, Yellow – *Secret Love*", "Cyclamen – *Diffidence*", "Grape, Wild – *Charity*". Then, like a foreign language dictionary, the second half allowed you to select a sentiment, and discover the appropriate plant: "Absence – *Wormwood*", "Fidelity – *Plum Tree*", "Meekness – *Birch*".

"Unfortunately, Robert himself put no signature or anything, in it; but I know it was his because, after his death, Stuart asked me if I'd like to select a few things from his bookshelves – my parents, certainly, had been fairly close to him – and ... there's something else ..."

"Yes?". She knew Bill was going to confide something intimate, secret perhaps.

"If, in the first section, you turn to Rose – it's underlined in pencil".

"*Love*".

"Quite. Just as he'd thought ... and just as he felt ..."

"I don't ... what?"

"Rose – had he got this book by the time he'd named her? I guess not ..."

"Yes, of course! His daughter ... Stuart told me ... she died very young ..."

"And like all such things, I don't think he ever forgot ... Don't mention this to Stuart, please ... I only discovered it – the Rose reference, that is – years after acquiring the book ... I wouldn't want ..."

"No, no of course ..."

"And there are other pages with delicate pencil marks at the top corners, just as some people turn over the corners of pages ... Yes, I think I said before ... things in Robert's work seem to *mean* something ... and flowers, perhaps, are one of them".

The phone rang, and Bill went out to the hall to answer it. This gave Daisy a moment to look for another reference in the little book, one more direct, personal; "Daisy – *Innocence*", she read; then, next to it – a strange feeling came over her ... a tingling in her spine – she saw a small, but definite pencil mark; *Yes, there was a reason ... **I** am part of this ...* But she didn't have long to contemplate it.

"Er ... it's for you ...", said Bill, returning. He'd shut the door behind him, but still proceeded to whisper – "It's Mrs. Levenham!"

"What, Stuart's wife ... Rosemary?" Bill shook his head, and mouthed a two-syllable word.

"Miss Taylor? Stella Levenham here. I hope you don't mind me calling you at Mr. Harvey's. Stuart – my brother-in-law – said I might reach you on this number. Could we meet?"

22

"Robert gave many of his works a title – did you know that?"

"No. No, I don't think I did".

"Yes – Stuart told me. Often, they're scrawled on the back of the picture, in thick crayon." *Well he never told **me** – does Bill know? If he did, he also didn't tell me ...* "Yes, here there may be a simple-looking picture of rocks, or a beach – or it may be a dining room full of the usual domestic things – and yet, lo and behold, on the back, it bears a name ..."

Mrs. Levenham – Daisy couldn't see it being *Stella*, at any point – had asked that they meet up in the small, pleasant, municipal garden or park, that ran alongside the main road, a mile or so from the town, in Carbis Bay, and fell down towards the sea. At the sides were several tastefully planted beds, and a few benches; but the scene was dominated by the vast expanse of blue sea that ran out to the horizon, a view closed only by the rocks and lighthouse at Godrevy. She was – Daisy had anticipated this from the way Stuart had spoken of her – a somewhat severe woman; dark colouring and wispy greying black hair. It was a warm day, and yet she wore a well-fitting skirt and jacket; it was as though she had just been at some slightly-formal event – judging a village jam-making contest, Daisy thought – but she guessed that actually, this was how she generally appeared.

"Yes, we have some of Robert's pictures ... Also, a few of his works bear a date."

"Yes, added to the signature, in paint."

"Quite. One of ours depicts this very place."

"*Here?* These gardens?"

"The same. Yes. The gardens, the flowers, and the sea. Obviously, the sea – vivid blueness – is important; you can see just how it dominates, here. Wasn't it true that you yourself, just now, looked more out to sea than here, at the land?"

"Well ..."

"But in our picture, though the sea is prominent, the principal emphasis is elsewhere."

"Yes?"

"It's *here*". Stella pointed downwards, to the ground they stood on.

Daisy was confused for a while. "The lawn ... the grass ...? Well, I suppose it is ... large."

"And what do you notice about this grass, as it is now?"

Daisy had no idea; what was this about? It was like being on trial, interrogated by a barrister or someone. "Well ... it's ... just grass ... green".

"Exactly, and very well kept – now, as probably then. *You* have the disadvantage of never having seen the picture. In *that*, it isn't merely green ... There are white dots in it, many of them".

"White ... dots?" *She must think I'm utterly clueless ...*

"The date, next to Robert's signature, is 1978."

The young woman realised. "They're daisies aren't they? In the lawn ... in the painting? I would have been just ... one ..."

"Yes they are ... and they led me to realise who you are ..."

"And – from what you say – I imagine there's a title written on the back? In crayon?"

"Yes ... but ..."

"It says *Innocence*, doesn't it?"

"Yes it does!" Stella was startled, for once thrown off her guard. "But ... how did you know? ... I can't think how ... You're a very intelligent young woman indeed ... But *I*, certainly, am not *innocent* ..." She turned to face her, and then, more than at any time, Daisy was aware of the dark eyes, hooded, like birds of prey were supposed to have. A certain sadness sparkled in them, along with something like confidence, endurance.

"When you first wrote to me, Clive had recently died ... it was still ... a shock. I sent a message to Mr. Turley, and thought that was that. It was only some while later – looking, as you realise, at our painting – that I thought of daisies ... and my late-husband's – what's the phrase? – *love child* ..."

"You ... knew about me? And you must have known my name, as well, to have realised from the painting ...?"

"Yes, I knew. Clive was not one who could keep things to himself ... indefinitely ... not the important ones ... It was, I suppose, that time – after seven, eight years – when a marriage goes slightly stale ... the boys had just gone to school ... his career had stalled a bit ... Yes, we knew about "Daisy". I suppose "Taylor" is your mother's name? She married?"

"Er, my father's ... well, not the real one ..."

"Clive never said anything about your mother ... well, perhaps that would have been going too far ... it was all long over, of course, when he ... a sort of confession, I suppose ... My husband was a man who increasingly, as time went on, needed ... pardoning, forgiveness ... that's the way it seemed, certainly ... I assumed – once I realised about you – that, now he was dead, you would be seeking ..."

"Look, Mrs. Levenham – I haven't come for *anything*. Well, just, perhaps ..."

"Yes?"

"I read an article in one of the academic papers, it was very ... bland ... Just, as you'd expect, academic stuff which, not being a scientist, meant little ... It would be good to know a bit about the real man – I mean, you've already said a little, but ..." But Stella geared herself up to say something else –

"It was I – I'm almost too ashamed to admit it, now I've come to it – who ... forced their way into your holiday flat".

Daisy gasped. "*You?* But ... ?"

"And ... the note ... Amateurish isn't the word! ... I just thought to slide it under the door ... but when I'd found the place – you gave your St. Ives address in that letter to me, remember? – I discovered an alley which led to a back door – french windows – and lo and behold they were jammed half-open already, just begging to be given a push ... but, then ... Crash! The *noise*! I was certain I'd be discovered ... When I'd ... left I went straight to the Sloop and drank a double brandy ... couldn't *believe* what I'd done ... you know, I almost went to a shop and bought cigarettes – I'd given up smoking twenty years past."

"So there was no "we" after all?"

"No, that was a ... ruse ... suggest there were several of us ... I suppose I thought I was being clever."

"Well it certainly frightened me! I assumed there were a whole gang – like I'd stirred up the Cornish chapter of the Mafia against me!"

"Miss Taylor ... I think this is the first time I ever remember feeling guilty ... utterly wretched ... and not a little foolish. It is now quite certain that had you been seeking ... recognition, shall we say, you'd have taken your opportunity and raised it with Mr. Turley ... Stuart convinced me that you were genuine ... told me about the University of ... Harpenden or wherever it is – does every tin-pot place have a university these days? – and the paper you're writing ... So I have to ask you to accept my apologies ... you don't *have* to obviously ... but I hope you will."

"Apparently he was an authority on the chemical reactions of the brain, or something?"

"Yes, perhaps the best there is ... *was*. I imagine your mother can fill out that a little ... I suppose her being in a scientific profession, also, was how they met. Look, to try to make amends, I've brought you this." It was a large dusty envelope, ragged at the corners, but once stout, the kind that has string to wind around a thick cardboard disc, to fasten it.

"Just a fortnight ago, James & James contacted me; they were Clive's solicitors in London – Carey Street, Lincoln's Inn. Hearing of his death had reminded them that they still had a box of Clive's papers which should have gone to Truro, along with the rest, when we moved down here. Most of them were copies of typescripts of his books, which Clive had left with them prior to the refereeing and publishing process – a wise precaution, he always said, against plagiarism – but they're all related to work published years ago, so there's no point keeping them. There were one or two other things that I'll pass on to Turley – and this."

"And it is …?"

"It was Robert's. I can't think *how* Clive came to have it, let alone deposit it with *his* solicitor. It seems to be a collection of bits and pieces he wrote at one time or another. Partly, I think it's what they called a "Commonplace Book" – it has poems and quotes written in it, from various sources, and one or two other things, much of which are too small to read, at least for me. One part might be a sort of diary. I suppose I should have gone through it but …"

"And you're going to give it to me?"

"As I said, to try to make amends. Of course, it will really belong to Stuart, now. Could I ask you to return it to me, so that I can pass it on to him? Shall we say, in a month or so? You've got my address, phone number? I'll somehow have to explain to him that you've seen and used it. Incidentally, I didn't tell him about the … you know … your flat. He and Rosemary consider me to be the black sheep as it is … I wouldn't want a reputation as a house-breaker being added."

"Well, I suppose real burglars – men – would have strewn my clothes about … and done worse things … at least you only tore a few books and papers …" Daisy said it almost light-heartedly – but Stella caught it, and fixed her sharp eyes on her.

"*Tore?* Damaged papers …?"

"Well, yes … but no real harm …"

"Miss Taylor – Daisy – let me assure you that I tore nothing, and barely left any obvious signs … except the … damaged door, and the note …"

"Then ...?" Their realisations were simultaneous.
"So there was ..."
"... was someone else there ...!"

23

A more complete and curious mixture of anxiety and excitement Daisy had never before experienced, and she could only neutralise it by putting the question of the other intruder out of her mind as much as possible, and concentrating on the book, and how to go about working on it. Should she share it with Bill, who would then become complicit in Stella's conspiracy to keep Stuart in the dark concerning it – albeit temporarily? Or should she simply keep it to herself, and plead a few days' work on her notes, in the spare bedroom? The reality was that Bill now knew enough to realise that her notes and papers were not such as would require more than a day to work on – mainly because of the little she'd so far discovered ... *but that is going to change, this is **not** going to be the same as Freddie's ledger* ... Thus, in the end, she came down on the side of telling him – but not about Stella's "housebreaking", concerning which she'd given her word ... besides, there was still the identity of the other intruder ... – *Oh dear! There it is again! Can't avoid it ...*

24

Daisy racked her brains, trying to remember her 'A' Level English ... modern poetry ... – but then turned the page and discovered it was T. S. Eliot; Robert had written it in – but not which poem he had been copying. He had also copied things she knew of – the rhyme about going to St. Ives ... kits, cats, sacks, wives ... how many people going ...? – and lots of other snatches, doggerel she couldn't recognise, some of it. But there was more of the modern poetry from major people ... and some quotes that came from St. Augustine and Kafka and others. Clearly, this man had had many interests, and was well read, educated ... Deciphering the diary entries was going to take longer, however (the snatches of reproduced poetry, etc., she noticed from a quick look ahead, seemed to increase as the book went on). It seemed as though he had just made the diary entries at certain times ... some periods of time were in great detail, but then it would lapse for a while, a long while, in some cases; and all of it was in tiny writing ... Daisy got to thinking that what she found were just portions of diary, transcribed from proper diaries into this book. But maybe that was wrong, maybe he just wrote during times that were significant or important to him ...

Bill had been simply amazed that Stella had decided to give the book to her. He, Daisy guessed, had inherited Stuart's view that this Stella was a cold fish, who was as likely to help an enquiring outsider like Daisy, or pass on the contents of her late-husband's document box, as she was to go around handing out five-pound notes to homeless people on the streets somewhere, or hippies in Penzance. Daisy realised she should have worked a bit harder at coming up with a reason why Stella might be in her debt, or ...something. Bill duly agreed to get his pictures off the wall (several were fixed with screws, some by his father) to look for titles on the back (he couldn't remember seeing any, but was open to the possibility, and his curiosity was aroused). She had settled into a sort-of routine at Bill's. From time to time, they arranged to eat together, but he always cooked, as that seemed to be one of his passions. Often they talked about Robert and his wife – his parent's friends – and Robert's later life, after Mary's death. Bill had once used to visit him regularly, apparently – Crowsavon being so near – but a while ago, that had come to an end; "The time came, when I seemed to be a source of ... well, he always got *very* agitated ... talked a lot, very loudly, about walking in Wales, seemed to think I was a companion, or one of his old art school mates ... started speaking in ... well, it might have been Welsh ..." Bill went out early most days, but she'd not enquired – and he had not offered – as to what he did for a living; it didn't seem to be the thing to ask. She, in turn, went off to the local libraries and museums – Newlyn, Penzance, Truro – trying, vainly, to discover some leads. But mostly, she studied the book.

"Surely they never know it, never imagine – the hundreds of tourists, I mean, people who come to the town for golden sands and bright blue water – never know how grim the weather can be, how … [some words were absolutely unintelligible; Daisy was going to have to just mentally fill them in, imagine]. Well, it can. In fact, much of the year it can be very grim, squalls coming in from the Atlantic onto this most exposed strip of land, a finger jutting out into the great ocean. A fair, southern climate, sometimes, yes – but racked with pounding waves, at others … crashing onto the shore, against the harbour walls. Walking along the Warren – past that low wall, directly beside the sea – you risk a drenching every time. But here, where we are, the sea does not reach us, the spray does not rise up. Here, there is the mist, the swirling whiteness – or blackness – that comes down sudden from the hinterland, or inland, from off the water. And then there's the rain, rain driven along in clouds, horizontal, almost, that straffes the windows and rots the wooden frames that hold them precariously, the wind rattling and buffeting them. There can be some filthy, harsh weather in Cornwall, as well as the pleasantness. Sometimes the bad, wet days run straight into the night, and darkness settles especially early; on such black, awful nights, I recoil from the storm, hide, almost, as best I can in the creaking house's least-damp place; but such is insufficient, insulating never my … [*soaked?*] skin from the fury without; the fury within swirls regardless; darkness comes to me, betimes, in every place I hide." Well, he had a way with words, sometimes, without a doubt – Daisy thought. She turned a few pages, strained, once again, at the tiny writing -

The cruel waves took you, my dearest,
And held you deep in their embrace,

> *And always I will know them as your vile abductors,*
> *Captors who stole you from me*
> *(My dear Love, I long for you,*
> *Will be with you, in time, eternally)*
> *Meantime, I must drag myself though the endless run of days -*
> *That dread, dull awfulness -*
> *Till I am beside you again.*
> *But, actually, those who stole you will keep you safe for me – warm.*
> *While time is, the Waves will be; but not Eternally.*

– at moments like this, Daisy felt like a voyeur, like one hiding behind a curtain while some pair of lovers spoke softly to one another, whispered, but in her hearing; but what was this? Who were *these* lovers (surely this was real, real people)? She felt her cheeks warm.

25

"That painting of a storm – the large one that was on the stairs – is there a title on that one?

"Took me ages to get off, it did, the screw head broke, the right one ... and I was balancing very precariously on the ladder. I tried to think where exactly Dad would have stood it to do this, the ladder I mean, and which ladder, actually ... they either seemed too long, or too short ..."

"Oh, sorry!" Daisy realised that she had started all this.

"No, not at all. Guess. The title, I mean. It's written rather small, actually ... no wonder we missed it ... weren't looking."

"Er ... *Storm at Sea* ... *Fog and Rain* ... No, *Darkness*, that's it!"

"Almost. *My Darkness.*"

*Of course ... the paintings are his experience, **his** feelings – not just depictions of things ...* The book's writings, or some of them, she realised, were going to be virtual descriptions of the paintings, or accounts, in words, of what he was aiming to depict, with the deeper meaning hidden in both but revealed a little more explicitly in his prose ... and perhaps in his poems also, if the "dear Love" words were anything to go by. She was sure she'd glimpsed more poem-like things ... now she was surely on to something *really* significant, had solid documentation, evidence of how he felt, and the importance of his works ... or some of them. Without a doubt, there were paintings that had gone, moved far away from anywhere that they could find them – he had, after all, sold a few in his lifetime (she thought of art-loving holiday-makers taking them back to London or Yorkshire or somewhere) and she had no reason to believe that those few were not important also, or that he'd hung on to the significant ones – and some pictures (she knew from looking, as she was now able, at both sides of those in Bill's collection) bore no title or descriptive writing at all.

Some entries in the book were just lists and notes, things she couldn't understand. Some were certainly accounts, and details of expenses – pounds, shillings and pence, money seeming old-fashioned to Daisy. She couldn't make out anything as to the actual items of expenditure (the writing, where there were notes, was far too small); and maybe it didn't matter anyway. Perhaps he'd been writing out the details of the household bills. (He'd tried to be a full-time professional artist, but for a lot of the time that hadn't worked, and it had had to be a combination of casual jobs, and Mary working; Stuart had been sent out on paper rounds and suchlike, he'd told her; at times they'd been appreciably poor, though he hadn't used the word). One piece of writing clearly involved notes from railway timetables (journeys from Exeter to Bristol, then to Cardiff, then Swansea; change again for Carmarthen ... she hoped trains were reliable in those days, whenever it was – there was no date, as with most things in the book – since the next train from Swansea, she saw, was more than an hour later). And there were – she'd half-expected it – shopping lists, at least, artist's shopping lists. At this time, he was clearly preparing his own boards, no longer using canvases (though he surely would have done at first), but he still used varnish and a mawl stick (with *his* size of work?). And here she found reference to the etching Bill had spoken of, that time he'd first come round – plates, acid and ink were required (Bill didn't have many etchings, and to be honest, she'd thought them a bit of a disappointment, lacking the power she found in some of the seascapes and depictions of rocks and cliffs; in them, he seemed preoccupied with groups of fishermen who seemed to be sitting around idly, curiously purposeless).

26

"Crying, constant crying, noise, endless noise … however could S. cry so much? Most of the day, it had gone on, and all of the night. Mary was beside herself, also weeping, lying head buried in the bedclothes, sobbing, shaking … and S. grizzling on, with no sign of stopping. And outside, a very dark night – darker than normal, it seemed – and the rain lashing down. I walked up and down the landing, holding S. in both arms, with the hope that I could, at least momentarily, soothe him, quieten him just for a few minutes, time to try to give Mary a little respite, peace … but it could not be. R. was not like this at all. I walk up and down, the screaming striking my ears from separate places, and the thought in my head that I alone have sanity, strength, I have not given up to wailing, raging despair. But I *might* … it could easily happen … *I must not go mad! I must not go mad!* Soon, I give actual voice to those inner words, the voice that I have so far kept within me, *mine* … *I must not go mad!* – I am shouting, as those around me are mad, maddened by noise, grief. The rain is clattering down still; the noise is continuing … I am going … I am going … "

Daisy heard a tap at her door, and knew it was Bill.

"Yes?" He entered, carrying his latest piece of retrieval.

"What d'you think this picture is called? Guess!"

It wasn't large, and showed a table set for tea, with flowers in a glass vase, and nothing but the most usual tea things. In the background – it was like a photograph whose focus was only on the table – a dresser was suggested by a few swift strokes of dark umber, with lustrous shadows hinted in dark purple.

"Er ... *Time for Tea? ... Shall I be Mother? One Lump or Two?* Sorry ... I'll try to be serious ... It's an iris, the flower ... er ..."

"You'll never guess ... look at the decoration on the china."

"The pattern on the cups? ... Just a paisley whirl, isn't it?"

"*Seahorses*. Yes, that's what they must be."

"Oh ... yes. You don't see those often, as pottery decoration."

"That's what I thought. And I also, if it's any consolation, had no idea what they are until I read it – and I've had it on the wall for twenty years ... more, probably ..."

Then Daisy looked at the crockery more carefully. Next to the cups there was a glass sugar bowl ... and that had a seahorse etched on it as well. It was one of those pictures where the light is deceptive. She knew of many where pools of darkness lit up a few foreground objects in brilliant relief, dazzling *chiaroscuro*; but here, it was as though the technique was reversed, with a rich, suggestive hinterland – seeming, at first, to be the dark area – but subtly revealing sombre gloom around the tea things.

27

"It was a miracle, I suppose, the fact that I had fallen asleep in my chair that night, and hence, that I was there when it happened. A rosy glow – beautiful, perfect, just like those sunsets off Land's End – I had dreamt it, well, half-awake, snoozing, that state they describe as between sleep and awakening, when a person is half in one, half in the other ... <u>This should go on and on</u> – I had perhaps been thinking. Fortunately, the waking part of me surfaced, took over ... Where was I? What was this? I surely looked horrified – at the fire – I started up ... it was coming from the fire-grate, red flames, and now choking, black smoke billowing into the room. It must be some kind of chimney fire. Fire! I shouted to Mary and Stuart: "Mary, get the boy out of bed ... get out into the street ... Never mind the dressing-gown ...""

It's a warm night. I rush into the kitchen, thinking to get some water (<u>Is that wise?</u>) Fortunately, I stop to drag away the rug and the chairs ... I run to the hall, grasp the phone, phone the number, hands shaking; I was dreaming, beautifully, a few minutes ago ... ("What on earth? What is it?" – Mary is shouting from upstairs. "The fire ... it's all ablaze. Get out into the street ... with the boy ..."). The fire brigade should be coming, now. No. The rug – on the fire ... I am rushing back to the room, handkerchief over my mouth ... grabbing the rug with my left hand (Heat! Terrible heat! – It forces me back ... I can't ... I try ...). Finally, I am managing to throw it down onto the flames ... its impact makes sparks and smoke shoot out at me ... now I'm retreating, rushing back, hoping my efforts are working ... Certainly, it looks better, now. Out in the street I hear noise ... it's Mary ... "Flames? What flames? Chimney?" – I shout. Flames leaping ... the chimney-pot, outside – she's saying. But inside, it seems to be dying down a bit, controlled ... The fire brigade are coming, I tell her, yes ... Is the boy safe? Yes? They're coming ... Not long ... "

Daisy had never been in a fire, well not actually *in* one – but she had been near to one, the house across the road when they'd lived in Tottenham. She, also, had awoken with a rosy glow filling her vision, seeping into – or was it from? – her dreams. Mother had cried out; they'd got out into the street, but there was no danger to any other properties. They'd just stood and looked, in silence, after a while.

28

"Mary, shouting ... that's the first thing I knew, knew about. She didn't just whisper (thinking that that way, if we were quiet, silent, we could disturb him, overcome him somehow). She must have become conscious in sleep of a moving around, downstairs. Perhaps it invaded her dreams ... and they can end violently, vigorously ... the clatter and bang she gave to her summons, her rage; and it tore awake, of course, the realisation, following soon, that I had to get out, go down, face it … him … Fortunately, there was a bolt on our door; I told Mary to fasten it after me, secure herself. Her cry, earlier, had surely alerted him, he knew that we knew of his presence. Nonetheless, I was as quiet as could be. <u>People are supposed to pick up the poker, aren't they?</u> – a curious thought, at this time; <u>by the time I'm down by the fireplace, I might have come up against him</u> … I walked carefully around the passage, down the stairs hoping not to make the steps creak (Did any of them squeak or move? I hadn't ever known, noticed). I got downstairs, looked around, parlour, kitchen, front room, breathing as quietly as I could. I looked everywhere. Nothing. Then back upstairs – a little less cautiously, now. So, bedrooms. We had had Stuart in with us, in his cot; for once – once, mercifully – he slept soundly … From, inside, I could hear Mary breathing hard. Then I thought … a terrible realisation hit me. I had tried everywhere, looked everywhere – except one place. Rose's room. I go there now; prepare myself, that is where he is hiding. For once, I think, I wish I did have a poker. No matter, must be done. I turn the knob carefully, risk the creaking as I open Rose's door carefully. The curtains are as we have them most times, open. The moon is shining down through the window, the room is fully bright. I realise – with a sudden fear – that he might be behind the door. But I remember that Rose's door opens right back against the wall; hesitantly, breath held, I am pushing it right back to the inner wall; it is creaking badly, now. There is no one behind it. I am looking into the room openly, now, not trying to hide or disguise myself. There is no one in it. Just an empty room, forlorn … emptier than if someone – a child, perhaps – had just slept away from home, one night, leaving her things strewn around her room in the speed of packing; oh happy mess, infant clutter! There is none here! But no intruder, no one pouring out drawers and cupboards, looking for aught (and he's not under the bed – I look down there – because a while ago we took away the mattress; no need of it). I am calling to Mary (yet still in a subdued voice) that there's no one in the house. Well, not now. The sound of Mary pulling back the bedroom bolt. I am going down again (not listening for creaks, this time). The back door is open. The radio-set has gone. There *was* someone here. Mary's cry must have startled him, caused him to rush off. I am walking up the stairs calmly now. I am passing Rose's room. <u>Stuart will have to move in there, soon. Too big for the cot before long. Rose's room</u> ... "

It sounded as though Stuart was a baby, or very young, Daisy thought – before her mind was flooded, without any warning, with dread, fear even ... the second intruder ... who could it have been?

29

"How long! How long will it be like this! (Will it always be so? Perhaps it will).

Failure, that's what I mean, failure, hopelessness "

It had been very tempting to dart from one place to the next, to seize upon parts which were more legible – wherever they were located in the book – and read them first, leaving the more difficult bits till later; but all Daisy had read and learned about research – learned, also, by mistakes – was that you had to be methodical (and she couldn't forget her mother's words, from childhood: "butterflies and daisies, butterflies and daisies ... you've got a butterfly mind ... flit from one thing to another ... you were well named!"). Thus, she stuck rigidly to the self-imposed rule to work slowly from the beginning to the end; but it certainly seemed that Robert hadn't acted in this way. His use of the book appeared to suggest that he had opened it at times – well, more often than not – randomly, and used any available empty page, sometimes missing out two or three, and some of the gaps seemed to be filled in later, if the handwriting was a reliable guide; and, for Daisy, there was a lot more of the book to go. Above all, she hoped there might be some kind of real end, that he would finish at a *proper* finish, conclusion, not just break off like some second-hand paperback in a charity shop that has had its last chunk of pages drop out, or one of those modern novels never really finished, inconsequential. At this point, the thing seemed to have taken a turn; a turn for the worst, perhaps. Previously there had been many recollections, memories of difficult events that had been very real to him, clearly, as he wrote; but now it was rather more about his thoughts, accounts of his inner feelings, confessions, even, and they weren't particularly optimistic. Once again, Daisy felt like a silent observer, unseen, as though she was not supposed to be looking in, listening. But he had chosen to write these things down – why? And why – as Stella had asked – had they found their way to Clive? And – she'd never thought to ask this before – did daisies attract butterflies?

"Every attempt I make – every one – ends like this … the people who don't bother to write back, or don't return the submissions, just nothing … many times, it happens, many times. She looks at me reproachfully, quite often. Yes, I know it, see it. She doesn't mean me to see it, but I do. How can I go on? How can *we* go on, like this? Not now the boy is with us. When R. died, it was as though it was some kind of … well, sign … some kind – it's terrible, to say that. I had to persevere, had to go on … and on, and <u>on</u> … Why did she marry an artist? I want to say that to Mary: Why? <u>Why?</u> But I don't. I can't help it. Help what I am. Can't. Sometimes I wish it were different. Wish I wasn't."

Now, in these passages that Daisy was currently reading, he seemed to be preoccupied with failing, failing to create a reputation, or any kind of mark. Failing to make a living.

"Don't get me wrong, I <u>have tried</u> (I wonder if she realises that fact? Knows?). More than once I've packed my things away, resolved to get a "proper job". Well, that's what they're called, isn't it? She must have realised <u>that</u> part of it, me going out early that is, several days on end – no one can live in secret, keep everything hidden – I've admitted about the job, whatever it was, has been. I've several times thought to be a fisherman – did she realise that, I wonder, I mean, really know that that wish was inside me – rather than just being one of the various things I've thought I should turn to, this painting being so ... hopeless? But it never lasted, never ... This "proper job" thing ..."

"I know who I am, what I am ... if only because nothing <u>else</u> works ... I kept getting drawn back to it ... driven ... It's just like the tides, the sea that pulls away from the shore ... but it always returns, can't help it."

Poor Robert! More and more like, this, Daisy came across. "I'm such a failure that even my attempts to give it up – art, that is – have failed – <u>that's</u> how much I've failed!". And again: "I read somewhere the other day that every life is ultimately a failure ... in the end ... Nobody does everything they've planned to do, they leave off with a dozen ambitions never fulfilled ... always meant to do ... <u>something</u> ... but never managed it ... all their early dreams – so fresh, optimistic, hopeful ... but only fulfilled in part. Those places they wanted to go to, things they thought to do ... security they meant to create in old age, a nice place to end up in – but only half managed it, if that; the recognition that it has all been useless ... But <u>my</u> life has been failure not just at the end, but all through."

Daisy got to wondering about *herself* ... where, exactly was she going, with all this ... art history, teaching ...? What was it all about, everything?

30

As she walked around the harbour, later, some words of Robert came to her ... something about looking at the small children on the beach (he can't exactly have been old, his own child Stuart must have been quite young), seeing in their faces so much merriment and joy – free, totally, of thoughts about what they might become, where they were going ... Also, Daisy had come across a sort of chart or plan which had a column of initials and then dates, with Xs beside them in a further column, far right. She realized, from things he'd written, that he had been sending submissions of some kind, presumably to galleries or agents, people like Bernie no doubt ... though whether to places in London, or locally, she couldn't tell. The dates seemed to refer to the 1970s. Presumably, he'd go in person, locally, just posting things further afield. Indeed, he'd made lots of attempts, if this was anything to go by, if she was interpreting it right, to establish himself, to find a better footing.

Bill had urged her to spend more time out and about, sightseeing and relaxing; not too much time indoors (she countered that by saying she had a lot to do, a lot still to go through, she'd promised Stella not to take too long; soon it would be the end of the summer ... not that long, now). But on this day, she'd taken his advice ("On Porthminster beach, go behind the beach shops and toilets, across a small public garden – a few flowerbeds and small shrubs, really – and find a narrow path that winds upwards, to a bridge over the railway line, and up into a broad lane – a clutch of nice, recent houses on the seaward side, with car-access, so look out for traffic – then follow the lane – down a bit for a while, then very steeply up. You'll come to a public shelter that's attached to a little house that's boarded up, the Huer's cottage, where they used to look out to sea, for fish schools, and signalled to the trawlermen in the bay – there's a plaque about it. Keep on, it goes down again, then the lane broadens out. You can keep on that path – Hain Walk, it's called – until you get to Carbis Bay, *or* you can branch off to the left, towards the headland – several paths to choose from – but be careful of where you come out onto cliffs, and steep rocks going down to the water's edge").

Daisy took his advice, and soon was having a pleasant walk towards Carbis Bay, first looking at the plaque on the Huer's cottage, then wandering on. The path broadened and started gently falling, the tall trees forming a solid canopy overhead, sun glinting through the leaves, yet too dense they were, in places, to fully admit it; on a *very* bright day – which this was not – this was be a very pleasant place to be, and while it was not unpleasant now, soon she knew she'd want to leave it for one of the paths that peeped out from trees to her left. And then she began to see pathways down to large houses, set towards the sea, places, surely, where the well-to-do of previous times had spent large family holidays, nannies carefully coaxing young scions from the water's edge, folding them into bed in make-do nurseries until next day's excitement. The path she chose soon moved through the large bushes, and emerged on the headland, grass beneath her feet, and the far, bright horizon beckoning. She saw Godrevy lighthouse, and the bright cliffs and sand of the shore beyond. Walking a little to the left, she could see the town and the harbour, the headland beyond, jutting out. To her right, below, there were not cliffs, but rather rocks sloping down gently towards the sea.

She went towards them, looked out, and down, to the incoming tide. She saw where streams were running down across the rock, covering the surface with green sward, making them appear, even at this distant, to be treacherously slippery. She saw, then, groups of children gingerly clambering across them, bent, it seemed, on skirting around the headland, at this low level above the sea, treading on exposed rocks only, intent, seemingly, to navigate this way to the town. When she ventured a little further down – the children had passed, now – she saw that the edges of the rocks descended into the water itself, though some of them seemed to run straight down towards small inlets with a sheer drop of a metre or so, down into deep water, that churned and gurgled into dark recesses it had carved beneath the overhangs. Daisy strained forward, and looked intently, experiencing an attraction – yet aversion – to the fascinating, rugged shoreline ... and at that moment found herself, suddenly, inexplicably, a little faint, light-headed ... drawn, yet wary, repulsed ... She sat down on the grass, instinctively, wisely, in some instant act of self-preservation against danger. She could see how someone – she'd heard of such things – could easily fall, perish ... Bill had warned her. She got up carefully, and then walked back to the town.

31

"Of course, trying to give up doing what I've been doing for so long makes me face all kinds of things, ask all sorts of deep questions – particularly, why exactly I'm doing it, what it's all about. Yes, of course, I can always say this is <u>me</u>, this is what I am, the way I'm made – not my doing, was it, that act of making? – and now, I'm just following what I'm meant to do, meant to be ... what I <u>am</u> ... working out this inevitable, unavoidable <u>me</u>, despite all its bad consequences – and they're many (like being hard up all the time, having to put Mary and the boy through it, through something that's not <u>their's</u> – this is <u>my</u> burden). But mainly it's the failure, that awful experience ... Couldn't I have been a farmer, say? I'd have loved being out in the open air, working under the skies ...

"Why, after all, entertain the idea that things have to be represented – <u>re-created</u>, almost – in order to be made real, or experienced ... why does light, shadow, texture, any of those things, have to be reproduced with this curious sticky stuff? ... other people don't feel the need to do it – they just enjoy the sunshine, or watch the sea ... walk along a country path and let their fingers run through the long grass beside them ... why might it be that some of us – me – have to go about recording it, whatever it is ... and why should such a simple need as this (if this is what we have) cause such unpleasantness to all around us, and ... to me – such pain, the pain of rejection, <u>constant</u> rejection? Besides, so easily the result becomes bland, lifeless. How can <u>I</u>, anyone, reproduce the foreboding drama of glowering skies, the quiet anger – resigned, defeated – of the dying sun ...? And in any case, who wants all that, now? All people want today is television ... and all the "art" there is is just nastiness, weirdness – why do people want to create sickness? Isn't there enough badness in the world, do they want more? Why? Yet this is the way I could be led, into ... strangeness ... What would old DT have thought? Thought it odd, perhaps that things had finally come round to that way ...? And Mam too ... "

This was it! *Definitely*, at last – a reference to Daniel Titus, sure to be! Now all Daisy had to discover was how he knew, or had known, Titus (at University College, the enrolment records of the Slade had had no such person, before or since Levenham's time). But this was a definite reference to him ... but just who was 'Mam'? Titus's mother, presumably. And all the ponderings about what art was about, and especially in the present time – well, Daisy had come to expect *that* at some point. Robert Levenham might not rate anything as a modern artist – but at least his musings – questionings – were those of someone who actually practised art, unlike all the theory people; academics mostly. But then, some while later, she felt there was something unexplained, something bothering her ... a strange, physical feeling. It was early evening, and, alone, she had cooked a basic meal. Bill was out, as he often was, in the evenings. Maybe he was a big Freemason, she found herself thinking, and this was Lodge night. Then again, he could be one of those volunteer lifeboat men, right this moment wracked by spray as his tiny vessel rose and fell against the crashing rollers (she'd heard a siren or something, sounding from down in the town, or the harbour; it wasn't a particularly pleasant night). She'd thought to get a shower, change, and wander down to Fore Street, but now it was raining hard. Still, have the shower anyway, she decided. Soon, it was water falling over *her*; and as it did so, she realised: *I could be led into strangeness* ... Why 'I'? What ... *strangeness*?

"Of course, the fact is that some of these images are extremely beautiful – not mine, I mean, but really great paintings, and not only the great ones ... the best produced at any time in history, really; even today. To capture the ripple of light across the landscape, the light that reflects off a calm sea ... the amazing colours that flow from flowers ... from them, out of them … out into the world … delicate, sensuous membranes, so easily crushed, so brief in their glory, their life faded in a day or so … I have tried, <u>tried</u> to recreate that … and the point is, that even if the result is always eternally inferior to the reality, the world – people – need this reality before them, need to have it fixed in an especial moment (such that an actual flower can rarely do). Does the world need ugliness – of the kind that so many of our "great" modern artists produce for us? I think not. If they want ugliness, they don't need art, pictures; why might they? They only have to look into the human heart – their own, preferably. Might I make that journey, turn back into that sad, depressing way? Perhaps. Was that all it was about, the long struggle through life?"

Wow! – that's all Daisy could think. It was beginning to get late. Bill had not returned, she thought, otherwise she'd have heard his key in the door. Time to get into bed; soon, wouldn't be warm enough to be able to do this, sit about in just a dressing gown. She'd begun to see it, feel it, the summer approaching its end. Although she didn't have to get ready for the new term, or anything, she'd really have to work a bit faster; she didn't have for ever.

32

It was perhaps because Robert Levenham was ~~in career terms~~ outwardly ~~such a failure~~ experienced total lack of success that he was able to objectively evaluate the mainstream (one even might say establishment) art of his time, and openly articulate ideas concerning it, albeit in the privacy of his commonplace book. Hence, his writing is of a ~~decidedly~~ thoroughly meditative, fragmentary ~~kind~~ variety, and not any kind of approximation to a structured aesthetic …

Daisy was trying to write again, this time burning, almost, to record the thoughts and ideas that Robert seemed to *throw* out, his feelings and reactions getting the best of him.

… a direct response, his ideas, perhaps being the equivalent of primitive or naïve painting compared with the brittle ~~thought~~

intellectualism of the avant garde. Naïve art – so respectable, of course, now, among the Modernist establishment – actually subverted Modernist abstraction by its totally direct depictions, much as RL's <u>private writings</u> subvert the high culture of the oh-so-respectable ~~middle-brow~~ avant garde ramblings ...

"Realisation that the root of the word *poet* means to be a maker, the maker of a <u>made thing</u>, should cause us to see that any kind of art must be the making of something – painting also. Now, just look at the painting that you see around you, things – visual things – that have been *made* in recent times ... what kind of making has that been? In paintings of mine, I have tried – at least tried – to make something of goodness, or at least, things that are at worst neutral, not bad ... but <u>ugly</u> art, that is the making of something bad – well, evil, actually. It is <u>not</u> just the business of not making anything at all; for evil is not insubstantial. Of course I worry about the world I will go into, if I go this way; but he tells me there is no chance of that. I suppose I have to believe him. It makes me think – following from his words – why Dali called that one painting of his <u>The Persistence of Memory</u>? Did <u>his</u> remembrances recur, revisit him?"

Daisy was more perplexed than ever, as she read on, abandoning writing efforts with – once again – a creepy, uneasy feeling (like a snake, she thought, slithering up her body towards, her head, her brain) that she knew far, far too little – about Robert Levenham, his work, his circumstances ... When did this passage date from? Who was this "man"?

33

Daisy realised why the fishermen in the etchings seemed idle, listless (Robert had depicted them brilliantly, actually, revealing their mood and manner; "body language" was the key): not resting, relaxing, but without work or purpose, no point in anything (at first, she realised, she'd undervalued the etchings; it was good that they were readily viewable, that she could just go back to them; not much longer, though – she must go home soon …). Presumably there had been some kind of depression in the fishing industry, at this time, whenever it was. And she knew what it meant, what the etchings were actually talking about, depicting, Robert's constant preoccupation: failure, purposelessness. And shortage of money. She'd read about another, much earlier, downturn in local fishing, and what it had led to. When was it? – the end of the nineteenth century, the collapse of the fishing in Newlyn, near Penzance. People had turned to metalwork crafts, making beautiful bowls and dishes in copper, and shells and fishes culled from the world they knew, beaten into the bright metal. It had flourished, and today the Newlyn copper was valuable, no doubt in museums … What had Robert turned to, on his inability to establish himself, make a successful name, career … the crippling paralysis of failure, obscurity …?

34

"They talk about people sleeping peacefully. They mean quietly, silently almost; but you can always hear a soft whisper of breathing if, lying beside them, you listen intently, hold your own breath. But here, she is sleeping <u>absolutely</u> silently; no one will hear her murmur again. But I <u>did</u> hear her gasping, groaning, gurgling … they are not sounds I will forget. Here, in this place, though, I can almost suspend memory – recent experience, that is. Here, now, the past, though fresh, is firmly in the past; I'll never manage to recall it. Would I could, would any of us could! I would trade the ability to recover the past for the awful prospect of knowing the future – the worst of it would be there with it, including the bad which is now mercifully hidden. Recalling the past might give the chance to act differently, change choices, avoid accidents. Accidents … ! On the beach, the distant sight of the lighthouse was compelling, mesmerising you might say. I think even Mary looked long at it, looked out across to the far shore, seeing – as you always seem to do – a bright far horizon, with the sun gilding the bright, white fringe that skirts the land. Of course, she had toddled towards the stones and rocks, and small sandy cliffs that close each side of the beach (that to the west, towards the town we'd just been in, buying rock; somehow, that to the east (or is it north?) is never quite so attracting, despite its small headland church poking up, calling, competing). Of course Mary followed her. We scrambled onto the rocks, and walked along the flattish parts, me helping Rose across parts of it. Where we settled seemed very flat, and safe – no greensward, or water, no drop into the sea beyond, and the tide yet to return. Later, in the water, I struggled as best anyone could (Mary shouted out, screamed). Best is never enough. I shall always be that frantic person, there, struggling in bitter water. I shall never be the person before, buying rock and postcards in the town's shops.

Now, occasionally, I hear Mary sleeping quietly, peacefully (do I do that ever? Shall I?). Today, in this chapel or whatever it is, she lying here, I hear only my own breath, heart. I was not forced to come here. The past cannot be recalled."

She'd never been ready for this, despite all she'd learned. Daisy had thought that at some point she would come across a specific account, or reference to Rose's death, but hadn't expected anything like she'd found. Somehow, she *had* got to thinking of a tragic accident or something like that, not just illness (very rare as a cause of infant death, surely; so many tragedies, one heard of). Maybe it was time to flick through the later pages, she thought, jump ahead; there wasn't *too* much to go, now – but no, take it as it comes, stick to what he'd written as it was there before her; there might even be a reason why he'd interleaved memories and suchlike, confusing – to *her* eyes – the chronology. This passage she could securely date, 1963, but the bits before and after it were surely much later. There was no way he'd not have written about this, about Rose's death, she reflected, something that had lived on with him; but considering the way it happened …

"I believe strongly, <u>strongly</u>, in beauty, order, simplicity, and goodness; but I know well that when things are very bad, when you're <u>down</u>, for some very good reason, then beautiful things are somehow of no help; one cannot cling on to them, hold them to oneself, warm oneself by them … they don't help – however much they should. You are alone. And producing fine things, owning lovely things – seeing beauty in things – does not pay any bills. And, beside all my convictions, about art, goodness, and loveliness, I am not incurious; I do not lack pragmatism. I <u>do</u> wonder about it … what it would do, what it would be like …"

Then, three blank pages further on, her heart quickening, Daisy got some kind of definite information as to what 'it' was: "I looked long at it, when he first brought it – but there's little to see. It's just a colourless liquid – could be water. He had a sort of flask, no doubt from his laboratory. It is the door, apparently, the gateway. "Why not take it yourself?" – I asked. "Oh I have" – he said – "but for an <u>artist</u> … a man pre-occupied, strongly so, with beautiful images, sights …" Apparently you just <u>drink</u> it, simple as that … just swallow it (no syringes or anything). I can imagine a bright, clear, glass, and in it, this 'water' … and from it …"

From downstairs, Daisy at that moment heard the front door open, and Bill come in. Almost immediately, as chance would have it – he can't have got his coat off – the phone rang. Quiet, almost muffled speech, she heard, no doubt Bill asking who it was (it wasn't particularly late; rather, she'd turned in early). Bill climbed the stairs and tapped on her door. When she emerged, dressing-gowned, he said quite conspiratorially that this was, again, a woman, for her, "but not … that previous one". Bill was wearing a very dark suit, Daisy couldn't help noticing, before she went down to discover who the mystery woman was.

35

Well, it *had* been a surprise to hear her mother's sudden decision to have some time away, "And what better place than St. Ives?".

Was there any particular reason? – Daisy wondered, but, no, her mother had seemed to be holding nothing back when she'd said she just felt like a break, and it had taken only a few arrangements to get leave from work (most peoples' holidays were over now, it seemed) and make reservations. So, the evening after tomorrow, they would meet in her hotel, and then get a meal out somewhere (must remember – she thought – to look for a suitable place, ask Bill, perhaps). Such thoughts took from her mind the obvious questions, that stood up against her like a mountain, a rock face, about this substance, and this man … which – curious, this, she thought – she had a reluctance to probe. She had wanted so earnestly to learn about Robert Levenham; now, when she was on the brink of real discoveries, secrets, she flinched backwards – while also attracted … like the rocks running down to the sea, at the nearby headland … dizzy, just like then, she felt, knowing somehow that she would discover more than she'd imagined … and … it might concern herself … But there was just no reason at all that it would necessarily involve *her*, she had no cause whatever for suspecting that, but …

"Yes, it's right, right what he said; I <u>have</u> given much thought, contemplation to beautiful images – sharp of him to pick that up, really; I'd not thought of my brother's intelligence, brilliance, and all the rest I'm so often hearing of, taking that particular form, seeing into my thoughts, sort of thing. Yes. Yes, he's right … "

So that was it! Clive! There was something of his doing here, which had affected Robert somehow!

"What, exactly does it consist of, this ability to make lovely things, and the strange loveliness that is brought into the world, by way of them? Is it originated by … by whoever <u>makes</u> this thing you see before you, this image? (I think of something like the Turners, in the Tate … haven't seen them for years, but I'm still in awe of that … that light … sun … darkness …) Did <u>Turner</u> make them, truly – I mean the painted images? Actually, I don't think he did, really … No, he just brought them into the world … If not him, then perhaps someone else would have … But what will I bring back … from that place, from beyond those doors, those gates of uncertainty, questing … By way of this … stuff …?"

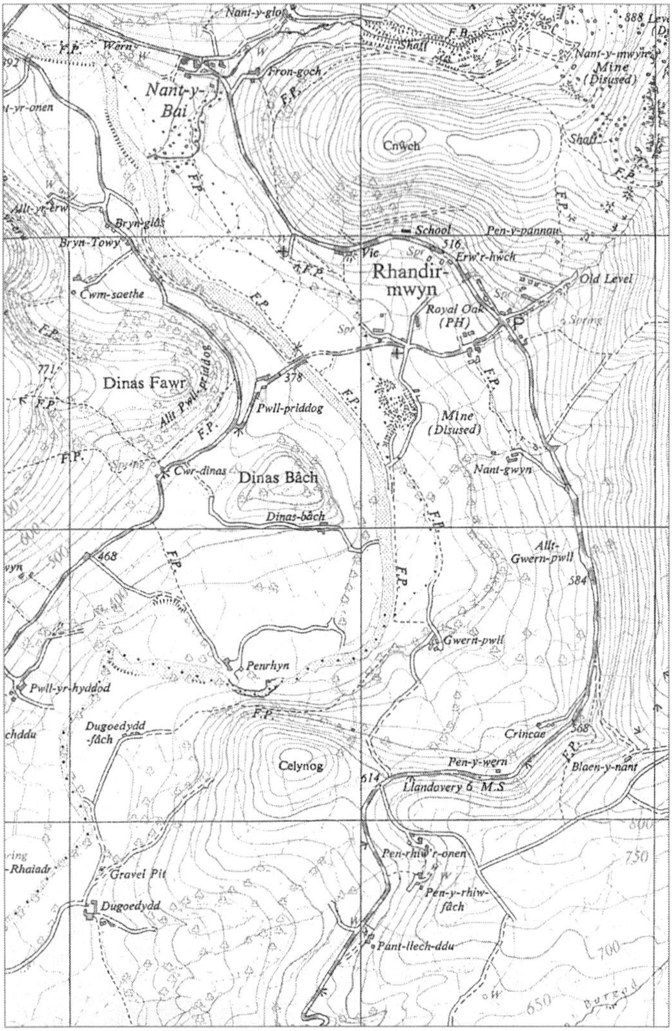

Nant-y-glo
Wern
Fron-goch
Nant-y-Bai
Shaft
Nant-y-mwyn Mine (Disused)
Cnwch
Allt-yr-erw
Bryn-glas
Bryn-Towy
School
Pen-y-pannau
516
Erw'r-hwch
Vic
Rhandir-mwyn
Old Level
Royal Oak (PH)
Cwm-saethe
Dinas Fawr
Allt Pwll-priddog
378
Pwll-priddog
Mine (Disused)
Nant-gwyn
Cwr-dinas
Dinas Bâch
Dinas-bâch
Allt-Gwern-pwll
584
468
Gwern-pwll
Penrhyn
Pwll-yr-hyddod
Dugoedydd -fâch
Crincae
568
Celynog
Pen-y-wern
Blaen-y-nant
614
Llandovery 6 M.S
Pen-rhiw'r-onen
Gravel Pit
Pen-y-rhiw-fâch
Dugoedydd
Pant-llech-ddu
750
700
650
F.P.

It is curious, my inability to reach any conclusion regarding the summit ... any definite decision, or firm view. It was all I wanted to achieve, experience. And yet still ... still I am not certain when, and whether or not, I arrived there. Hours, days of tramping uphill, bending my body downward, forward, towards the goal, the objective, my mountain-stick pressing firm into the loose earth (which is what it had become, the stones and scree left behind). I got to thinking that even the sheep had not ventured this high, nor any animal life-form that I could discern (I remembered, with some affection, the lumps of droppings – sheeps', and I suppose rabbits' – that been so common earlier; I had learned to tell, at a moment's glance, which could be burned on the fire, and which were too moist, too new). I suppose there must have been a time when I ceased climbing up and the path became level, and then, soon after, when I was descending; you would think my limbs registered some kind of difference, a new, fresh pattern of tension and hurt; a new ache. One thing I know for sure; there was no moment when I stood at the very top and surveyed all around (I had imagined a bright world seen from its roof, as it were, my gaze scanning all around, seeing the whole as all one, a unity compromised only by the inability to see all directions – for no one is omniscient, I knew). But that did not come to me, no; except, perhaps, in my mind.

And then, much later, I was firmly conscious of descent ... And now – forget the uncertain past, the lack of success, the not knowing – down, with certainty, to Crowsavon.

36

"A man's life – what he really is, he himself – is a mystery, a thing hidden, veiled from everyone, known to none. However much he says about himself, or writes down in diaries and suchlike – writings like this – no one really, <u>fully</u>, knows him ... perhaps not even <u>himself</u>."

Inside, Daisy groaned ... this was just what she herself had been beginning to think, a thought that brought something like dread ... and here he was writing it out for her, making it explicit, definite, unanswerable ... so she couldn't avoid it, hide, refute it ... maybe she'd never crack it, this art of ... summing people up, displaying, in a few apt words, just what made someone tick (today it was Robert Levenham, but in the future it might be ... others ...). She thought how top-rank scholars captured – *encapsulated*, that was the word – the subjects of their articles and studies, in just a few apposite phrases, such that readers thought to themselves, *Yes, that's exactly how xxx is ... what a brilliant analysis! What a clever writer!* But they would never say that about Daisy's work. And – she thought further – perhaps he's challenging me, taunting me even ... me, or whoever he thought might read this ...

"They say how today art has to 'reflect society' or something, show us all how we really are ... comment on modern life, and suchlike. Oh really? Why? And what is this 'modern life', 'present reality' etc.? Well, if they choose to 'reflect' the worst – as seems to be the case, mostly – all they're doing is making sure it stays the way it is, confirming it ... making it acceptable, the norm ... If they choose to reflect the badness – as so often, surely – they're just displaying the darkness that lies in the heart of man ... every man, everywhere."

It seemed that in this part of the book, she'd hit on Robert in a philosophical mood, although she was sure that these passages were not written at anything like the same time – the handwriting was too different for that. Some passages were becoming quite difficult, interspersed though they were with intelligibility – with seemingly-earlier writings. Perhaps he'd tried to write on the same sort of themes, in the same parts of the book, despite the different date ...Time's passage makes us all a little ragged, thought Daisy ... *goodness, Robert would approve of that!*

"I try to make images of the commonplace, but of the goodness and splendour that exists within it, that is here, all around us, if we can but see ... if we <u>will</u>, if we <u>will</u> <u>it</u> ... perhaps ... perhaps this "hydralisg" (as he calls it – often!) will open the door to seeing it whole, complete (he claims this is the effect). I am not a person who avoids experiences, strange possibilities – though I sometimes fear them; in a word, I will try anything (nothing I have tried so far, or done, has had much effect. It is bright, shining, I have noticed, a kind of clear crystal-like water)."

Later, Daisy could only think of this moment as like the experience of being hit in the face, or having the earth open under her ... *hydralysg* ... She knew this, had known of it, seen it. It was (she thought, at *that* moment) like having a desire to be sick ... or scream (in reality, she sat glued to the chair, behind Bill's father's desk). The silver, snail-traces, drawn in varnish ... the big picture at (what had it been called?) Darren's place ... this is what *they* had spelled ...

37

"We'd come up a long walk from the town, beside a road (fairly busy it was – even then!). Up hill it went, away from the coast, the sea-view, into a tunnel-like space – a great cathedral of branches – as trees rose up on either side, above us, around us. It was quite hard going, because she wouldn't stay in the push-chair, had to be carried, or insisted on walking. The road gave out into houses on each side, a residential sort of place, but then, after a dip down, and turns, we were drawn down a pathway to the beach – yes, I admit I was excited also, the prospect of the soft golden sand, and the bright, warmth of the day. A stream ran beside us, and then high above, the railway viaduct. Passing under it, soon we are on the beach, and Rose scampers ahead. We do not worry; all is safe and calm. We walk, trample, over some large clods of grass and sand, until we come to the fine, flat crescent of golden beach that snakes away to right and left; and now it is the business of finding a place to settle us. We are drawn towards the left-hand side, and walk on a little, always thinking <u>this</u>, <u>here</u> will do, but then thinking that maybe that area a little further on is even more inviting. Finally, we settle. No, Mary cries to her, there's no point going further, no need. Down go all our things, and we start to seat ourselves (folding chairs), and unpack our belongings. It is a simple, ordinary scene; a few others – but not many – on the beach also; some have those wind-break things fitted on sticks, hiding their modesty as they change to their beach-clothes, or giving some privacy as they kiss, or sleep (we don't have anything like that).

Distracted with little things, it is a surprise, sudden, when Mary shouts to her, don't go on ahead too far. Not long, very little time, fraction of a moment, I am clambering up the rocks. I can't actually see her. She cannot have got up onto that overhang … surely not, sure … Mary is soon up on it. She's nowhere to be seen. We climb up quickly, rush over slippery rocks, not carefully, not quickly enough. She must be … must be … I am back on the sand, where the rocks begin, their slither down to the water from the high cliffs ending here. I am tearing off my clothes … she must be, can only be … I am virtually naked. I cry out … I am in the water, thrashing. I swim around the rocks to the left (I swim badly, hardly at all; not strongly). I am dipping regularly below the salty, bitter water, looking through the silent green to try to see her. I am spluttering, choking as I come up. I try this several times … I am clambering to other places … I am realising the hopelessness … futility …

I am back on the beach, standing, heaving, water running down my arms and legs. I scream, shout … there are people here … they seem to be taking hold of me … I fight them, thrash out … but there's no point, they're so strong … they hold me, take me … "

Frightening – a frightening immediacy, shocking sense of reality, the here and now, happening at this moment – was all Daisy could think. For a few moments, she sat in silence; but this would not do, she simply had to put the book aside, now, and get ready to go out. This was the evening that she was to meet mother, who, after the long journey from London, had no doubt had a few quiet hours resting in her room in the hotel, up Tregenna Hill. Maybe *she* could help …

The hotel reception had rung up to the room, and when her mother came down, she suggested that they have a drink at the bar before going off into the town to eat. Again, Daisy found herself wondering about her mother's seemingly-sudden desire for a short holiday – but she appeared relaxed, and not at all preoccupied with anything. Rachel had gone to the bar to order drinks, and, after choosing a table near the window which looked out across the bay, Daisy went up to offer to carry the glasses, while her mother paid the barman; as it was, she already had them in her hands. Rachel asked how her Levenham work was going, as they walked back to their seats.

"Well, it's certainly taken an odd turn or two …"

"Yes? Tell me?"

"Well, what, if anything, does … er, *hydralysg* mean to you …?"

Only Daisy jumped aside quickly enough to avoid all the splashes, as her mother dropped the full glasses where she stood. On the carpet, sinking in to the pile, Daisy thought they looked like splashes of blood. *However will they get them all out, clean it?* Rachel recovered herself, and returned upstairs to change her skirt.

38

"Tell me", Rachel asked Daisy, when they'd chosen from the menu in a pleasant fish restaurant in a side street, and the waiter had returned to the kitchen, "what do you know about LSD?"

"Well … er …", said a slightly-surprised Daisy, trying to remember, "Wasn't it that 1960s thing … West-Coast … junkies … acidheads … drugs, sex, rock 'n' roll … bad trips … or something?"

"It was actually developed in the late '30s, and not in California, but Switzerland."

"Oh …?"

"You have to know more than a little about LSD in order to know about hydralysg – if that's what you want … and, I think that's what you asked? Then, of course, I'll be more than a little interested to hear how you came upon it, and where it fits into your research."

"Oh … yes, of course …"

"A Swiss chemist called Albert Hoffman synthesized it, when working on a large research programme aimed at finding medically useful derivatives of ergot alkaloids, and amide derivatives of something called lysergic acid. LSD was first called LSD 25, as it was the twenty-fifth lysergic acid derivative of lysergic acid diethylamide – that's where the name LSD comes from, though, of course, he would have known it by the German version of the name. At first it was thought that it might be a useful circulatory and respiratory stimulant – an analeptic – but interest in it lapsed for a few years. Then in 1943, Hoffman began working on it again, this time taking doses himself which made him feel ... well, intoxicated, as though with alcohol, but, unlike with alcohol, he experienced strange stimuli of the imagination, describing it as a dream-like state. Next, however, he took a much larger dose, and then – can you believe – set off home on a bicycle. Apparently, while travelling very fast on the bike, he thought he was just stationary (presumably he didn't have to go down any of those Swiss mountains, otherwise we might not have heard of him again). Well, he made it home, but spent the next few hours imagining he was possessed by a demon, his neighbour was a witch, and his furniture was attacking him. A while later on, apparently, he began to feel better, indeed, good, very good ... experiencing amazing images, strange shapes and colours, and – significantly – ordinary sounds around him produced sensations of vivid colours."

"Isn't that like ... synaesthesia ... I've heard of that ... some people experience sounds – music – as colours and pictures and ... "

"Exactly, so it appears ... though in the normal cases – if you can call them normal – they occur naturally, without any kind of chemical stimulation. Well, at first it was thought that LSD had a role in the treatment of mental illnesses, and conditions such as schizophrenia, since at this time – *late* '40s, now – they thought that schizophrenia was caused by, well, chemicals acting in the brain, what we call *endogenous* substances, ones that were there from the beginning. Medication was devised aimed at blocking the effect of the LSD, and then, of the – supposed – natural causes of the syndrome. In the end, schizophrenia was found not to be caused in that way at all ..."

"But ...? Daisy had begun to wonder quite where her mother was going with all of this.

"Very soon, the Cold War was upon us."

"The threat from the USSR?"

"Quite, and the hunt was on for some kind of effective mind control drugs, sort of 'truth drug' for use in interrogations. LSD was a prime candidate. The Americans were quick off the mark, their biomedical people testing the drug on soldiers who – at the time – had no knowledge of what was happening to them, or what they were actually being given. Apparently they tested the drug throughout the '50s and '60s, though little can be definitely established now – the records were destroyed in 1973, deliberately, apparently. But it was not only the Americans …"

"No?"

"No. We started testing it on servicemen in the '50s also, again, without the subjects' knowledge …"

"That would have been at … that place you worked at … the one you can't talk …"

"… Even now. *Yes, it may have been there* …" Rachel's voice had perhaps gone quieter because of the approaching waiter, and when he arrived, she became silent. But how, thought Daisy, could any of this affect Robert Levenham, it was before his time, easily … ? But the sight of her sea bass – its aroma – took such questions, at least temporarily, from her mind. Rachel had settled on shark fin, which didn't appeal to Daisy at all. Their glasses were filled – white, this time – and the waiter retired.

"Apparently a young soldier claimed to have seen the walls melting, cracks emerging in peoples' faces, eyes that melted and ran down cheeks, and even a flower turning into a slug."

"But … all this would have been secret, wouldn't it? I mean …"

"Oh, the facts have only emerged recently, and there's been no official statement, or acceptance of any liability, so far."

"But … hydralysg?"

"I'm coming to that …"

In fact, Daisy had to wait while the shark fin was disposed of; but she had to admit that her own meal was adequate compensation for the wait, more than adequate.

"Well ... and now I have to talk about ... Clive. As I told you, your biological father ..."

Daisy knew this was not going to be easy for her mother. She made certain not to look her in the eye, but concentrated, instead, on her peas.

"Clive was ... well, from the beginning – it was just his nature – very ambitious, determined to make a mark, and make it quickly – well, I suppose we now know he hadn't got all that long ... I went to work at ... the place you referred to ... and he had already been there a while – six or seven years older than me, of course – *and* married. I knew that, I have to say, he made no secret of it. It was the mid-'70s, and I was twenty-two when I got the job – younger than you are now – well, a little. Actually, I'd heard of him back at university, when I was training, a few years before; even then his name was known, a high-flyer, you could tell ... I suppose that was part of the attraction ... Well, our ... friendship ... as you can imagine, blossomed. I was very much the new girl ... He seemed to gravitate towards ... newcomers ... Before long it was – what shall I say? – confidences, and first among them – I mean in importance, in his mind – was his great ambition."

"The FRS? Rising high in the scientific establishment?"

"Well, that, but there was a more immediate one. Perhaps he saw it as a route towards fulfilling those others ..."

"Invention of something new?"

"Yes, sort of. This was ... what, 1975 or thereabouts, and he'd spent three or four years, alongside his research and studies, immersing himself in rock music, alternative culture – as it was called – reading Timothy Leary ..."

"Who?"

"A '60s pop culture guru, deep into drugs, and particularly hallucinogens."

"Like LSD?"

"Quite. And, by the time I met him, he'd some while ago decided that his great work, that which was going to make his undying reputation, was developing something different, new – but, naturally, based on what had gone before."

"Hydralysg?"

"He was very proud of the name. In fact, I think he thought up the name long before having any specific method of synthesising the kind of compound that he was ... what shall I say? – dreaming of ... Dreaming is perhaps the *mot juste*, as well ..."

"So ... what does it actually mean?"

"It's not a truly scientific term, just a sort of mixture of existing terms, and a bit more added for good measure. But, yes, I suppose it works, sounds good ... like an advertising slogan, or brand name, I'd say – a label. Memorable ... and that's what Clive wanted."

"So ...?"

"Well, the *lysg* part obviously comes from lysergic acid, and ..."

"And the 'hyd'?"

"Simply from the Latin for water, you know, hydrology, hydrolysis ... You see, a quantity of LSD in a glass has a certain yellow or brownish tinge, depending on how much there is, but Clive's synthesis, hydralysg, is ..."

"Totally clear?"

"Yes. However much you put in a beaker or whatever, it remains completely transparent. He was very taken with that ... had quite a capacity for pride, did ... your father ..."

"I see! That explains ...!"

"Almost *clearer* than water ... it had a sparkle to it ... like gemstones – I once thought – that were turned to liquid by an amazing alchemist (such as I then thought of him) ... and there was more ... But you're going to want to know more than the meaning of the name!"

"Oh, yes ... I mean, presumably he tested it, and ..."

"Yes. Do understand, that you don't just discover, or create, something like this – remember Hoffman, with his twenty-five syntheses ... Well, Clive didn't have to go quite to that figure, but there were – I seem to remember him saying – about ten or so products. At first, of course, he was able to test them on rats ..."

"What?"

"You see, where we were, there were such ... facilities ... and in a previous job he'd had, there were many others. This was a time – you may not know this – when laboratories tested tobacco by using dogs ... dogs smoking cigarettes ..."

"Ugh!! But ... did he take it himself? Robert says that ..."

"Oh, I don't think so."

"*Really?* But ... what was the purpose of it, exactly? And how come we don't all know about it?"

"Well, it was something of a pet project – not official at all, and the Department might not have approved of it, if they'd have known much about it ... no, an interest on the side! And then, I think, what with no real test results ... I fancy he just moved to other ..."

"Everything fine for you, ladies?" They hadn't noticed the waiter returning, poised to scoop up their plates, and stack the emptied vegetable bowls on his forearm (how *did* they do that? – Daisy wondered), the plates in his left hand, condiments in his right.

"Yes indeed ... Daisy, will you have a sweet?" – but before Daisy could answer, the waiter had said: "Certainly Madam!", meaning that fresh menus were on their way.

Rachel began again. "Like many of these things – such as mescalin – the purpose, I think, was to increase human perception, as well as possibly to cure mental illnesses. I'm sorry, I'm revealing that I really always was a *bit* of a sceptic, where his hydralysg was concerned. Clive used to say that I had no faith – what was the point of being a biochemist if I did not believe that substances would one day be discovered that would alleviate psychosis? ...Well, maybe there might be some that will. But *this* ... much more, really, than being therapeutic, I think Clive knew that ... You probably know, don't you, that only a portion of the human brain is ever used? That our capacity for perception is limited, selective, and so much that we learn, our experience, is lost ... ? Ah! Thank you."

Once again, menus in hand, mother and daughter had their minds upon choosing; but after a moment Daisy could see that her mother had become uncertain, lost interest ... it was all a bit filling, stodgy – or bland (*she's not a trim forty-eight year-old for nothing!*); Daisy then began to feel awkward, not wanting to indulge in treacle tart when, after all, it was shortly going to be *her* turn to do the talking. Soon, Rachel was eyeing the waiter – "Thank you, but I think we'll just have coffee … and the bill, please".

39

"You contacted Stella!"

"No, Mum, she contacted me, she asked to meet me her here in St. Ives, which is where she gave me this … diary or whatever we call it. It's actually a Common-place Book, and – it was really very generous of her – we agreed that, before long, when I'd used it, it must go back to Stuart, as Robert's next of kin. Well, I suppose it could go back to Robert himself, but I think Stuart has to decide about that. As it is now, he probably doesn't know it exists. She had no need to act in this way." The burglary, again, could remain unspoken of, she thought.

They'd managed to find a quiet corner in the lounge of Rachel's hotel, and indeed, all of the lounge, itself, was virtually empty. A clutch of late-holiday makers at the bar were a bit boisterous, and if they came and sat nearby, Rachel said, they could always go up to her room.

"I'm sorry, you must think I'm a bit negative towards her … but I'm sure I don't have to tell you that my relationship with her – not that I ever really had one – has not been particularly warm … reasonably … I was always the other woman remember, the bit on the side … I don't blame her …"

"Did she … know, discover … early on …?"

"Well, yes, early on. Her beloved boys just off to – Sherborne, was it? – and then the discovery of … infidelity … No, I can't blame her at all … But this book, and the information in it? It doesn't sound as though it's all about art, to me, this project of yours. I'm wondering just what you've got into … Ever since you got that letter … But it was me, in reality, who actually started things ... raking up the past ... As we didn't tell you some while ago, perhaps I just should have left sleeping dogs ..."

"Mum, this is ... *yes*, this *is* about art, it *is* my research ... though I now know, with what I've just stumbled upon, that I've only just started the real work in the last few days. You know, when I started with this, Walter Higgins, in my department, said that there could be a PhD in it. Well, with what I know now, there certainly should be ... effect of drugs on traditional, realist painter ... Remember when I went to see Freddie Jackson? Well, at that time I was thinking this Titus person was just some other artist ... quirky, strange ... but now it seems they were one and the same! Think, Grandpa Bernie probably handled lots of Robert's pictures, and had never heard of the man ... and Freddie too ... What you've told me tonight unlocks several mysteries ... the fact that so many of Robert's works show an innocent-looking glass of water ... perhaps with a flower in it ... only it's not water, is it? And now I've got to find out about all the existing Daniel Titus's ... look at them seriously, now ... And the money – Freddie's ledger-thing suggested that some of them sold for quite tidy sums – where did all that go?"

"So ... I've really started something, haven't I?"

"Yes ... as I say, unlocked something ... a new beginning ... a new start ..."

"You'll have to show me this book".

40

Trying to get a bus or a tube ... Daisy needed to get home, get back up there, whatever she did ... Standing in the dismal streets, with the lamps dim above her, like gas-jets in an old photograph ... or painting ... what looked like a taxi came up the street, and she thought to hail it (despite having no money), but it seemed to turn into some kind of military vehicle – no windows, only slits, with guns poking through. Had to get home, had to ... Waiting for a train, but only along some disused rural tracks, where weeds sprang up and threatened to lash her feet, her legs, while rabbits in the dark hedgerows chortled, cackled, so it seemed, and grew in size, number, until the time for action ... And beside the street came Darren with a candy-floss for her, and she said I haven't had one of those for a long time, no, not for years, and a harsh bite of it cracked her teeth, and out they dropped, one, two, three, on the thin boards ... she ached, *ached*, had to sit down after tramping the stairs – had to; and as she gratefully fell into the soft leather, her frail body fell – fell, fell, fell ... She shook herself, looked out of the window. It was almost light. *Why do I always dream about trying to get home, having to go there, urgently ...? You were taking a risk, such a risk, telling Stuart ... you had no way of knowing how he'd react! He could have walked away, ordered you not to come near his family again ... claiming to be his cousin! ... Just a gold-digger, you! Common little ... And there is the question of this book ... how's he going to react to that? ... Not knowing ... not knowing the secrets, secrets about himself, that* you *know ... a risk, such a risk ... And the break-in ... the other person ... When you get back to Hendon, they won't want you ... someone else doing your work ... rationalisation ... cuts ... easily manage without you ... new people in place – won't recognise you ... finished ...* So often, after dreaming, she tossed and turned, lay, sleepless, in one awkward position or another, choosing one of three in futile succession ... and always worries – the four o'clock fears – came as though from another ... another voice ... It was getting lighter, brighter, as the dismal questioner rattled on ... Daybreak, soon ... not long ...

Not Long Now

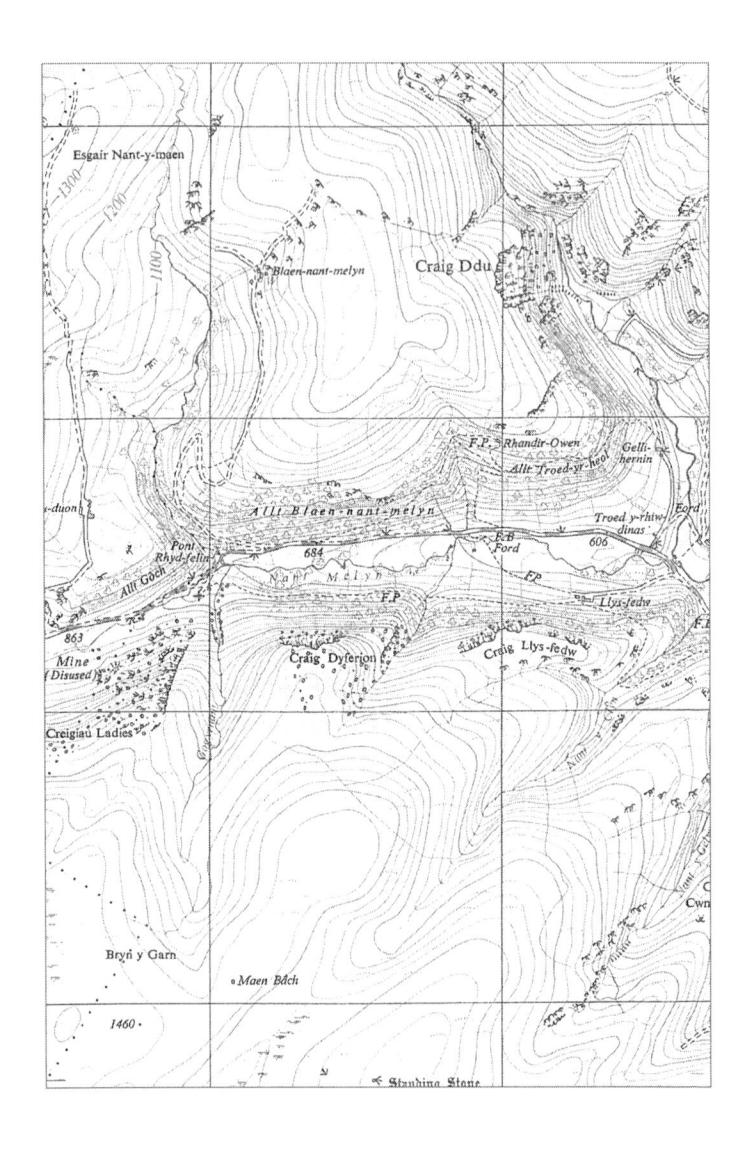

I was surprised by the difficulty of the descent. I had had the idea that this would be easy, the simple, welcome end after a hard climb; as usual on this expedition, nothing proved to be what it had seemed, or turned out, in reality, to be anything like what I had – for a long time – imagined. It was as though fantasy was now mocked by cruel reality, as though real life, and our coming to this moment, was proving quite the opposite of suppositions ... Experience is always a very different thing ... Today, reality just leaves yesterday's imagining in the cold outside, as though what we thought it would be (which now one only knows by memories) is inconceivable ... I cannot, just cannot, think anything like I once thought, or recall it; they are not even shadows, these far-fled dreams. They are not even remembered.

At first, we thought to descend by way of Craig-y-Rhaiadr – the rocky crevasse cut by Nant-y-Rhaiadr – a small stream it looked, on the map; but no doubt grew larger as it raced to the Tywi (it began its journey to the east, or north east of the summit, because I saw, on the map, how it curled around to find descending streams on the far side of Mynydd Mallaen, near where, in the youthful, hearty days of our journey, we had set out keenly up the hills (then, it would have been just a small brook; and such is how all great rivers begin, all great enterprises in the wide world). What I discovered, to my great dismay, was that the Craig was extremely vertiginous, and the river, though small, fell almost headlong, spectacularly, down into the gorge (above and beside the cutting, was the Craig Ddu, the map told us; presumably that means black *rocks, and certainly, as we looked at them from the ground outside our tent, they did look dark, formidable. (We had, at that point, decided to make camp for the night, and only attempt the difficult descent with first light; to try otherwise would be madness; I felt sure that the falling Rhaiadr would be spectacular, beautiful even, its smallness quite compensated for – but that sight was for the morrow, and besides, it must not distract us from our real business – to find safe paths to the plain below).*

Last night, in the tent, I heard it again. This time, the calling was like a soft music, a light tinkling that was so *quiet, not like a human voice at all ... but it was the same summons, identical urging ...*

41

So often, Daisy thought, this is the way it is! The very thing you're most worried about, lose sleep over, rights itself in no time at all; and an example of that was in the morning mail:

Dear Daisy,
I tried phoning you at Bill's, last night, but he said you were out. I had a letter from Stella, last week, and she explained about the Commonplace book, and of course, I'm more than happy that it should be with you. No, I had no idea that it existed, though Dad had said a few things about "I wrote it down" and "My book", which didn't seem to make any sense to Rosemary and I (I said about going through his papers, but I've never seen anything really significant, like this book). Stella said that she had no idea how it came to be with Clive's papers, but maybe that's a mystery that you'll get to the bottom of, along with others, as your work proceeds.
We're coming down to Crowsavon next week, and we must all meet up (Bill said, last night, that he would be very pleased for us to come to <u>his</u> place, though I know his work can call him out unexpectedly, particularly, apparently, at night). His cooking is a real treat – but I imagine you'll know that.
I'll phone next week, then,
  Yours,
  Stuart

42

All things considered, last night hadn't gone too badly, Daisy thought. Her mother was the only person new to everyone, but that didn't cause any awkwardness, and only once did Stuart and Bill fall into childhood reminiscences, but seemed both to sense that such things were better kept for another day. Naturally, there was much conversation about Stuart's parents, and Robert's art;

but of Robert's book, they all kept silence, as though they knew that mentioning it was raising the matter of Stella and Clive, spectres best not invited to this particular feast. The day before, Daisy had got a chance to speak to Bill, and said how she'd thought she'd not mention, to her mother, the matter of the break-in ... and realised how her erstwhile discretion was turning, if she did not check it, into entangling deception; he, of course, did not know about the *second* intruder, that Stella had posited – whoever that might be – and Stuart didn't know that Stella herself had been an intruder. Bill had produced an amazing rack of lamb – and he hadn't been called away to any of his mysterious nocturnal activities; no reference had been made to his work or occupation, and yet Stuart had said more than a little about what it was like being a local authority surveyor in today's stiflingly-bureaucratic environment. Back at her desk, she returned to the book. (She'd dug out a thicker sweater – definitely beginning to feel a little autumnal).

"There was more of it in the paper, today ... dead animals and things in tanks ...supposed to be art ... Ours is a society intent upon death ... When a people – its art – turns its back on the beautiful and truthful, and espouses this ... vileness, it is a sign of death, dying. This is what we are doing, dying ... there will be nothing left ..."

"Of course, naturally, in this society, all the nation's honours and positions – and money, of course – are given to those people who produce the most meaningless, the ugliest things. Of course, we should expect such a place to be accorded to such people, in our world – intent on destruction, as it is, decline – we should expect nothing else. And pathetic me continues trying to make these small images that capture only goodness – nature, its truth ... what a foolish old man! But, of course, the beautiful and the good come only from – speak only of – something higher, beyond us, beyond our world. Naturally, we can only deride it, disregard it – or rather, not see it at all; choose not to. Life, goodness, has left us. We have chosen death."

Not a good day, presumably, for Robert. Yet this same man had chosen (well, agreed) to test this drug, see what its effect would be … on his work …

43

Daisy and her mother had gone walking along the track, that led beside the beach and then the cliffs, that leads west from Porthmeor to Clodgee, and beyond. They'd been lucky, that day, with weather. This was Rachel's last day, and it was so good that – a little wrapped up – they'd managed to get a day's walking. Daisy knew that her mother wanted to talk; the night together at the restaurant, had left some things unfinished.

"I … I didn't mean to give the impression that Clive was … just led by dreams of a … *hippy* kind, you might say … all that expanding-of-consciousness stuff … that, yes, but … he was very idealistic – we both were – youth, I suppose … wanted to make the world better, for everyone – *everyone* – and science (that's what we all used to say, then) was the one and only means … All the Eighties stuff – individualism, wealth creation, all the rest – that was still in the future, remember …"

"So … what went wrong? I mean … Where did he go … what did he do, later …?". Daisy *really* wondered about the circumstances of their break-up, how it came about … and where *she* fitted in …

"There was, of course, something *selfish* about him – well, that's not the word, not selfish as it's usually meant … self*ist* – he believed first and foremost in what he was to achieve, putting that first … goodness, I bet Stella knows more than a little about that, learned it, over the years."

"His *work*? His work more important than … *you*?"

"More important than anything, anyone … perhaps – yes – more important than *himself* … Have you never met – say at Hendon – these 'My Work' people? If not I'm sure you will. Why, universities …"

"And that's where he went?"

"Not directly ... he was actually head-hunted, as they say – can you imagine? Getting a phone-call offering you a job? Name your own price? Well, it's never happened to me ...

"And you say that ... his drug receded somewhat – found another pet project?"

"Perhaps. And, of course, he gave a lot more to ... his marriage – I won't say threw himself into it, that was not his style with relationships – and, of course, I wasn't there to see ... but I imagine ... heard some things ..."

"And ... me ...?"

"I think when he clearly saw ... when I'd totally convinced him that I was going to make a proper life for us, together, alone ..."

"And ... er, support ...?"

"I made it quite clear that that would not be necessary, or acceptable, really ... things were changing with regard to ... single mothers. And, of course, before long, there was Dad – Trevor – around, and then things were different anyway."

"And so I grew up ... thinking ...?"

"But not unhappily, surely? We were, actually, a very good family ... certainly in the early years ... he doted on you."

"Yes. But Clive? Tell me more – if you know it – about his work, his ... ideas."

"His work, in as far as I know about it, concerned memory, and, in particular, the way synthesised substances could affect memory ... its structure and nature, particularly the long-term memory."

"Yes?"

"The effect of substances on the serotonin receptors in the hippocampus. There's the 5-HT2A receptors, which are the targets for psychedelic drugs, such as LSD – and that's where Clive's hydralysg come in ... The hippocampus is part of the brain's frontal lobe – called that because that's one of the things it looks like ... Greek for "seahorse" apparently, and ..."

"*What?*"

"Seahorse. The man who first isolated it considered it looked like a seahorse – it suggested other things to later people, but – you know how names stick. Nowadays, other than memory, several functions have been posited …"

"Seahorse? You know, in one of Robert's paintings, seahorses are used as a kind of decoration. I'd thought he'd got it from the copperware they made at Newlyn".

"What?"

"Yes, early in the century – well, the early twentieth century, I mean – or before, they made artefacts out of copper, at a place called Newlyn, near here … they decorated them with lots of fishes and, well, sea-life, that kind of thing … I thought Robert had got it from that. I've never heard of crockery decorated …"

"Crockery?"

"China, tea cups … At the time, I just thought it was the sort of thing he had in the house, used the things around him. Now I know that things didn't appear in his work by accident – well, mostly. *Memory* – so that's what Clive was concerned with …"

"Well, some of the time … as I understand it …"

Beneath them, below the cliff-tops they now walked along, the sea churned, and waves – some of them really large, now, fascinating yet frightening in their forcefulness – threw white spray up towards them, as though daring them to get any closer, as though striking at them, reminding them of an angry ocean's chaotic power.

44

"All day, the wind was getting up. By late-afternoon, it was really very strong – a gale coming in from the Atlantic. Stuart came home from school, and immediately went off playing in his den. It was the best Mary could do to get him to come in for the tea she'd cooked; he bolted it down, and then off again, back to the little house I'd built him at the bottom of the garden, next to the fence.

Well, the fence really formed part of it, two of the sides, at least, a very high fence, that closed the garden and gave us, and the neighbours at the bottom, some privacy. And the evening wore on, and, to be honest, I'd quite forgotten where he was. It wasn't dark; this was still late-summer, but my, it was windy! I look out of the studio window, upstairs, and see the trees swaying, violently, from side to side, the leaves stripped away as though it was Autumn, and the roar, the constant roar, rushes to my ears and seems to cut out any other sound. I see the fences on the right side of the garden beginning to rock to and fro. I wonder – worry – about the chimneys of the tall houses nearby, set up on the hill. Loud noises and rumbles are sounding, from all around. The fence at the garden's bottom is jerking violently, forward and back, forward and back. Now, I see it crashing down, and down onto … onto Stuart's den … He is there! He is in there! It's flattened, now. Mary! Stuart! Where's Stuart! Mary? I'm rushing down the stairs two at a time – mustn't fall, stumble – Mary! I can't see where she is. I'm in the garden … down the path, running … Where is he? I reach the pile of planks and posts, thrust them aside – the wind roars at me, almost as though to stop me in my tracks … spoil its sport … I am shouldering beams and struts and suchlike … here is Mary, she grabs some thick planks and suchlike, though the wind tries to clutch them, back from her; they are waving, flapping, as though trying to get free. I see him … he is crouching down … I grab him up … Mary is crying, shouting … we are running up the path, back … indoors … 'Why ever did you go down there on a …' But I am too relieved to scold. I hold him. Mary is crying still, now … I suppose, for joy."

Now, Daisy paid much more attention, than she had before, to when Robert wrote about some important event in the past. Her mother had set off, yesterday, for the long drive home, preferring not to break the journey. Daisy asked her why she didn't spend a night in Dorset or Hampshire or somewhere; but she wanted to get back as soon as she could. That night, Daisy dreamt she was being attacked by a clutch of grim-faced seahorses.

45

"He often phones me up, asking me how my thoughts are going, if I've made any decisions. 'Have I agreed', he means ... he's like a persistent salesman ... Maybe that's what he should have been, not a scientist, but a salesman."

Daisy found that these snatches of Robert's words were more and more interspersed with transcripts of poems, and other things, and much longer transcripts than before – Shelley, obscure Victorian writers (as she supposed them to be), something much older and archaic (Milton?). At first, she slogged through them, looking for clues (such things weren't her choice of reading, normally); but later, she got to thinking that – unusually, perhaps, for Robert – they had no particular meaning or relevance to his situation. It was as though they were hiding the personal revelations, the introspections ... serving as a welcome distraction for him, so he didn't have to think too much about this matter ... the matter, surely, of if, and when, he might join in Clive's "experiment" ... become a "subject" ...

"He came here today (it seems he and Stella are having a few days' down here, a bit of a break, apparently). He was pleasant, having almost an attitude of supplication ... but he so, <u>so</u> wants me to test his ... substance ('experience' it, he says) ... and there was a sting in the tale. He put it nicely, sure, but the meaning was clear. I'm in his debt – yes ... Think, he said, how only a few years ago – seems like last year, he felt – <u>he</u> had gone along with <u>my</u> wishes, come round to <u>my</u> way of thinking ... It is a kind of emotional blackmail, of course. But he's right. I'm in his debt. He did accede ...Then, it was me doing the persuading. And he did accept what I said, what I asked of him. He left it to Rachel, her wishes ... no more, for him, no more part in it."

A strange feeling came over Daisy ... and in her stomach, like sickness ...

"He told me a lot about it, what it's like ... but for someone 'of the eyes', of the <u>senses</u> – he said – it would be many times more so. Now, he said, it's he who needs my help, not as before, when I argued with him (I wonder what happened to the letters? I can't imagine that this was something he shared with Stella – actually, I don't think 'shared' is a word you would use concerning that marriage ... I might be wrong, of course). I wonder, also, if Rachel ever knew ... that but for my pleading (that's the word, really), she might have had even more of Clive trying to persuade her to ... end it."

Now, Daisy did begin to feel very sick, stood up, and unconsciously calculated the time to reach the toilet. She knew what "end it" could mean ... surely did ...

"It's like a debt, a big loan or something, without the terms of repayment having been settled. Now, he's come for recompense – put very nicely, of course. Well, I'm a man of honour, and he did keep his side of it – well, I suppose he did. I'm sure Rachel was a very strong young woman, but at times like that, in her condition ... who knows what might ...? And now the dear little thing is with us, apparently ... lovely name; reminds me of R."

There was a large flower-bowl on the chest of drawers, *jardinière – wasn't that the word?* Daisy grabbed it, just in time. There was an untidy pile of papers in it – they might have been Bill's father's, just left there. They wouldn't be of any use to anyone any longer.

46

Daisy lay on her bed for a long time. She began to feel cold; she couldn't remember having eaten, that evening. As often, Bill was out. Then, she thought – why not go out too? She got herself together, grabbed a coat and some money, and walked down to Fore Street. There weren't a lot of people about, and nobody lingering; it wasn't a particularly warm evening. She went into one of the pubs towards the beginning of the street. Inside, it was quite cheerful; not many people there, but music playing and a fire burning; it was early, yet. The pub was quite smoky. Daisy had heard it was likely that they would ban smoking in pubs. Certainly, it was grim eating in some of them, with smoke wafting all around you, coming home with your clothes smelling ... but who cares? – she thought. The pub sold wine by the glass, and she had a glass of red, knocked it back, and then – slower this time, staring into the flames – drank another. The barman gave her a knowing look as the third was being poured. Only when a man came up to her – *Alright love?* – did she realise that she was on her fourth ... *Might as well have bought the bottle!* ... She glared at the man, who disappeared ... *Did* your *father try to ... stop **you** being born? No? I don't suppose so* ... She got up, unsteadily – she'd not anticipated it would be like that, hadn't thought of its effect – and wandered into the street. She walked up in the direction of the Sloop. Time seem strangely stretched – ages, it took, to get to the street's end ... past souvenir shops, art shops, shops selling fudge and pottery, shops with little jars of scrumpy and liqueurs ... pasty shops ... on and on, until she came to the harbour-side, the harbour's end, where the long, thin wall snaked, over arches, out into the water. She passed it, kept to the roadside, and walked further, along past more shops and houses, on towards what seemed like another beach. A path skirted the beach itself, with beach buildings and huts on her left. Small waves broke on the sand, very quietly. It was deserted; except for a evening solitary wanderer, walking slowly with walking-stick in hand, prodding shells, and a way off, a dog running wildly, seemingly fetching sticks, and swimming into the silent foam.

Ahead, above her, a large mound loomed, some building at its summit – silhouetted forms that were jagged, hard, compared with the soft lines of the rising land. Soon, the beach and its huts were behind her, and she was walking on the mound itself, but it seemed terribly, wearyingly, steep – as she felt now – as though she had set out on some precipitous mountain – in darkness – and alone. Here she was, dressed as though for a stroll in the town, but entering into a vertiginous climb – as it appeared – as though intent on reaching the house, or whatever it was, that rose up before her, that seemed to call – to one who had strayed from the path of normal things, to be carried up, away … Daisy began to feel very tired, and she knew that walking *around* the hill was easier, less challenge there … and thus she came to that part furthest from the land, where the earth and grass beneath her feet began to sink down, inviting, pulling her, almost, to its outer edge.

There – almost a surprise, it was – she saw the land fall quickly to the sea, saw the glint of lights far out across the water … saw the lighthouse spray its familiar beacon, searching around the bay, like some far-away watch-tower that threatened as it sought to aid. And the waves breaking on the rocks, below – they seemed harsher than on the nearby shore, deliberate, strong, not flaccid, slow, somnolent. A curious whistle, they seemed to make, a following rush as they drew back, each crashing attack recalled in ordered withdrawal, not panicked retreat, with a fresh grouping ready to assault, behind. Gazing at the swirling waters – picked out in *chiaroscuro* as the far-light's glinting struck them – Daisy's swimming brain felt her physical self dissolve, each part of her substance weaken … She seemed to see bright lights in front of her – of a non-natural kind – like seeing stars, as if she had been hit about the head, got up too fast. Below, the waves churned against the stones, and foam thrashed and parried as in some bitter conflict, violence against the earth beneath her feet … pulling her, drawing her on … Her vision of the world turned and turned about, so that she knew no more what was sky or sea … and solid land had slipped away, silently excused. When, in a moment, she was standing no more, the batter of the ground against her back did little to recall her … and her crumpled form slithered down along its damp, grassy track, accelerating towards its- watery end.

Daisy was conscious of a thing moving beside her, a noise it made, chaotic, threatening, yet solid beside the flowing sky above

– darkening, it seemed, the last glints of daylight vanquished, dying; now, the thing tugged at her … sharply … sharp teeth … the jaws, surely, of that grim fate that waves had dragged her to …

"Ditch! Sitch!". What a strange thing to shout, Daisy thought; Witch?

"Ahh!" Another cry – though only distant, they both sounded, her muddled mind and senses quite separate, so it seemed. "Ahh!". *What were these strange noises?*

"Are you alright? Hello? *Can you hear?*".

Daisy realised a figure was set over her, leaning down, below, its wet mouth now groping at her face, teeth not far away …

"Mitch! *Stop it Mitch!* … Hello? Can you speak? Are you … did you fall?" Daisy found, actually, that she *could* talk. "Imagine … *nothing* … *nothingness*…What it is … We all know this … inability to remember, recall … that *nothing*, before, before we *were* …"

"Don't … don't try talking …"

"But … to have no … no *after* … by which to know *before* … *before's* nothing …*nothing* …". The person was grasping her, now, drawing her up …It *was* a person, she was sure … thought so, anyway … *But then again, she'd heard of people who thought you could have memories – well, they could – from the womb … memories, feelings …*

"Let's … let's just get you to your feet … there's a path, here …". Once the person helped her (held her?) upright, she was much better … the world as it was *meant* to be. The person urged her to walk, to move a little, with its support. Meanwhile, the yapping creature took to whimpering, no longer the keeper of the quarry it, unaided, had found.

"There we are … the path … Let's get back to the town … Yes, slowly does it, now!".

Clearly, the person had seen a bench or suchlike, sat her in it as she recovered somewhat. It was a woman who had found her – presumably, the person on the beach – or rather, her dog.

Daisy let herself be taken – firm arm, under her shaking arm – back the length of Fore Street, and then, despite protestations, up the hill – it seemed such a long walk – to her very door. Only there, with many thanks and assurances, would the dog-walker let her go, say goodbye. Only then did Daisy look into her face, her eyes ... what was it she saw there? What was it? Something – strong, significant; engraved, sharp, on her brain – but what, she could not guess.

47

Bill was in – for once, when she had thought to go quietly upstairs; sleep – and there was no disguising that all was not well; no possibility of silent entry. She let the door crash open, for a start, failed to hold it, then, lurched towards the coat-stand, making a clatter. Bill came out from the kitchen, whence smells suggested he'd been making some dinner.

"Daisy! Whatever's wrong?" She breathed alcohol all over him, muttered a little, lost for words – then felt ashamed.

"I ... I've had a ... bad evening ..."

"Come in, lie on the sofa ... Let me get you some tea ... and how about some of this spaghetti I've just ...?"

"No ... really ..." She'd thought for a moment of spaghetti, and felt sick. "Just a little ... tea ... thanks". Then, a moment later, thought how she *did* feel hungry.

"Have you been ... to the town?"

"Yes, sort of ... I had a glass of wine or two, in a pub ... went walking up a big grassy mound beyond the harbour ..."

"The Island".

"What?"

"Remember me telling you? It's called the Island – but it's not an island, as such ..."

"Slipped down on the grass ... falling – think I was, anyway – towards the sea ... Nice woman with a dog picked me up, walked back here with me ... looked strangely at me ... Nice dog, really ... if you like ..."

"Well, thank goodness you're back safe now ... Walking by the shore in the twilight can be dangerous. Here's a warm drink."

"He wanted ... He wanted to kill – well, a- abort ... That's the word ... me." *I can't think why I said that ... Something, something about this man ...*

Bill nodded gently, looked at the ground.

"Yes, my father – the real one, that is ... The book ... the book told me ... Robert recorded it – not outright, explicit ... but ... incontrovertible"

Indeed, something about Bill's manner – and Daisy barely conscious of it – made her talk and talk. He seemed to sink into the background, as though not there. And then she cried a little.

"The ... the last few months have been ... such ... a *shock*!" She didn't know how long she talked, but at last, she began to feel weak (*Should have accepted some spaghetti ... well, a little*). She knew it was time for silence, sleep ... time to climb the stairs. Suddenly, as from nowhere, Bill – reading her mind, perhaps – produced a big bar of chocolate, thrust it into her hand.

48

"I'm really glad you were able to spare the time ... to see me ..."

"No, my pleasure." Stuart could see that Daisy was not quite the intense, single-minded 'investigative art historian', intent on her quarry, that he'd first met, a couple of months or so ago. Then, she'd struck him as care-free, assured; even the evening they'd all met at Bill's, a few nights ago, she had been relaxed – but not now. "And as I said, it has to be today, really – we have to go home very soon. Management team meeting, on Thursday ... Have you come to a crucial place in your work, or ... some conclusion ...?" He'd come to St. Ives, from Lelant, to meet her, and fortunately they'd chosen a cafe that was almost empty.

"Well, not exactly conclusion in the sense of *end* ... but certain ... significant findings – things I should really make you aware of, if you're not already ... tell you about."

"That sounds serious! I'm sure there can't be anything, well, *grave*".

"Er ... to jump straight in ... It seems certain that your uncle Clive persuaded your father to take ... to experiment with a substance – drug – he'd made ..."

"*What?*"

"Things he confided to his Common-place book – the one Stella loaned me – along with some things my mother told me of, the day before yesterday ... Well, they make it certain that ... Well, that he agreed, after some persuasion, to try ... use ... this substance. Clive – my father – from early in his career, well, student days probably, dreamed of creating a sort of hallucinogenic drug ... And within a few years had the knowledge ... and the means – facilities ..."

"What? *Father?*"

"Yes ... and it seems he developed a rather strange painting style, under its influence – nothing at all like the manner we know him for, or subject matter ..."

"But ...? Where are these paintings? Why did none of us see them?"

"Well, that's part of it, really – if my hunch is correct. He seems to have developed a sort of separate persona under which he – or rather, the persona – painted these very odd things ... and none of you ever knew anything about them."

"No, I'll say not!"

"He had an alias, 'Daniel Titus' ..."

"Now ... half a minute ... Didn't you ask me about that name?"

"Yes. I'd come across it in London, my grandfather's old partner referred to it. Of course, the fact that they are the same initials as *mine* seemed, at the time, to be pure coincidence ... I've found no suggestions that they're not, as yet ... but I don't think so."

"So ... you ...?"

"Clive had been fascinated by LSD, in his youth ... all that psychedelic, flower-power stuff. His own drug – rather later, of course – had a name that made reference to it. Does 'hydralysg' mean anything to you – I guess it doesn't!"

"Not a thing!"

"As I said, the name alludes to LSD – Mum pointed that out – and the clear, water-like appearance of the stuff, *hydra* ... But I think it also tells us something else. Mum hinted at more, and, stupidly, I was too slow to take it up, enquire further ... I shall be asking her about it shortly, but my guess is that the 'hyd' bit is also a subtle reference to 'Mr Hyde'".

"As in Jekyll and Hyde?"

"Exactly. Artistically, you only knew the Dr. Jekyll; but hydralysg released the Mr Hyde – Daniel Titus. But I wouldn't want to push that too far, since Titus was hardly an artistic equivalent of somebody who roamed around back-streets doing abominable things ... But it did turn Robert into a man who *did* do things, artistically, that he would have loathed when himself, when in his right mind."

"But ... these Titus pictures?"

"It seems many were sold through Bernie's gallery – that's my grandfather, dead now, and I don't think we'll get to the bottom of that one."

"But ..."

"I think you explained that there was a time – in the '80s? – when he was fairly secure, materially ... Perhaps some of Titus's earnings ...?

"Perhaps ... And, of course, I wasn't at home during ... all this ..." *Odd ... Disturbing ...Unsettling* – Stuart couldn't be sure which word described his view of the things that Daisy had shared. He could see, though – from the way she breathed deeply, seemed to brace herself a little, that there was more.

"Was there a time – do you remember – when you played in a wooden den in a storm ... as a child ... it collapsed ...?"

"Yes! *Vividly* ... I was five ... You discovered *that* ...? It was in that book ...? Was he keeping it in those days, writing things down then?"

"No, not in those days, if you mean back then when you were five ... My guess is that he wrote it much, much, later."

"But ... why ...?"

"Clive had said – your father recorded this, certainly – that the drug would release all kind of ... aesthetic sensitivities, perceptions and feelings that were usually hidden ... above and beyond the normal ... And perhaps it did, but I think it's chief effect – this is just me guessing – was that it affected *memory*, and the perception of memories, and their location in time."

"Reminded him ...?"

"Well, not ... as such ... Stella told me, that day in the gardens, that Clive was known for his work on the actions of chemicals on the brain. Well, I fancy she was talking about his, shall we say, mature work ... but it was firmly based on his early ... ideas and attempts – which produced hydralysg ... hydralysg affected the hippocampus, that part of the brain that's supposed to control memory – control, rather than store – a fact which Robert seems to have been aware of. When under its influence, my guess is that he did several things. Sometimes he painted – as you say, you weren't around to see him – sometimes he wrote ... and ..."

Stuart got a curious feeling ... couldn't name it ... *Something big's coming* ...

"That business about your father ... Found in Carbis Bay in the late-'90s ... with no clothes ..." He was right.

"Robert was not simply ... *mad*, demented ... He'd taken off his clothes, most of them, to make it easier to swim ..."

"*What?*"

"This is just my ... my idea."

"Why ever should he have wanted to *swim* ...?"

"He was trying to rescue Rose – your sister".

"But ... but ... Rose had died ... *decades* before ...!" Stuart's head was whirling ... Really – could any of this *really* be ...?

"Not for Robert ... not at that moment ... Now, I don't know any of this for certain, obviously, but his accounts, writings ..."

"In the book?"

"Yes. His accounts there, they always start as ... well, memories, set in the past – past tense – but a bit later ... it's as though the thing – the drug – has ... taken effect ... I've read some of them over and over again ... In the end, in the last sentences ... he's there, right *in* it, amongst it ..."

"Sort of ... re-living it?"

"Exactly. And these, remember, are only the ones we know about ... have records of. My guess is that if we could collect a lot of the Daniel Titus paintings, well, we'd possibly find all sorts of clues to ... things that happened in his past ..."

"Significant, important things?"

"Traumatic events, yes. I mean ... in the book, there's an account of a fire, a burglary ... *When* he wrote it I can't be sure – but, whenever it was, he was *there*, definitely".

Stuart noticed that his coffee, undrunk, appeared cold – probably Daisy's as well.

"Shall we go and walk around the harbour?", he suggested. It had been dull earlier, and, he thought, looked like rain; but now the sun was shining.

49

"Your father ... I don't know how aware of this you are, maybe keenly, maybe ... He clearly mourned Rose's loss for a very long time ... never ceased to, perhaps ..."

"Well, I see it, now, yes ..." Stuart thought of disconnected snatches, that he'd heard at Crowsavon before, or Rosemary had recounted. "Are you thinking, perhaps, that in some way ... you, er, your father ..."

"He and I have never met ... in no way did he know me, as an adult, *or* a child".

"So ...?"

"I think it's most likely that he was quite closely in touch with his brother, say in the later-'70s, and then afterwards, also ..."

"But ... I'm sure I wasn't aware of it. What had they in common?" Strangely, perhaps, while Stuart had felt no unwillingness to question her earlier – perhaps fantastic – ideas, he was beginning to wonder if she was now straying from reality somewhat.

"What", she said, "they had in common ... or rather, *not* in common, was that Clive was going to be having a daughter ... sorry, I don't mean to suggest that I think Robert didn't love his son ..."

"No, no of course not, and besides ... I know he did".

"Yes. But, as we agreed, he still felt the loss."

"Yes. But ... there's a lot of supposition here ... It requires him to have been closely in touch with his brother – living in London at this time, of course – to have heard about Clive's ... forthcoming paternity."

"Yes, a lot of speculation. Perhaps when Stella discovered about me – as she seems to have done – she told ... your mother? As you say, supposition, guess-work. But *then* – I think I have to tell you this ..." Again, Stuart noticed Daisy gearing herself up, breathing a little heavily. "It seems certain ... that Clive tried to persuade *my* mother to have ... a termination ..."

Stuart could only gasp ... no wonder the poor young woman felt stressed!

"And ... from something he says in the book ... Actually, I really think I should have talked to Mum about this, before talking to anyone else ... His words ... the book ... make it seem that he, Robert, persuaded his brother to drop the matter, deter her, maybe ... When I first met you – rashly, surely – I'm like that, sometimes ... I told you that Clive, your uncle, was my father ... but, perhaps, I owe ..." Stuart saw it, before she said it. "I owe my life, perhaps, to your father!" Stuart couldn't help it, a tear formed in his eye.

They walked on in silence, setting out along the harbour wall. Boats of all kinds were tied up to it, with part-time sailors busying themselves, in the sunshine, with jobs they had to do on deck. The gulls cried and swooped. Stuart imagined one of them dropping a dollop of what seagulls drop, down onto the bright rails and newly-varnished woodwork, of a smart-looking yacht they passed – perhaps while the proud owner's back was turned.

Stepping carefully over tie-ropes, they then walked back. Daisy changed the subject slightly.

"There's lots of bits, in the book, where Robert expresses his ideas ... speaks his mind. I've really enjoyed reading that ... so fresh and different ..."

"Really?"

"Yes, his idea that beautiful things, beauty in art, are ... greater, bigger, than mere mortal creations ... That such things ... well, reach beyond themselves, or any of the people who – supposedly – make them ... Tell me, was your father ... a *religious* man?" He could see that, the moment she'd said it, she regretted it, understood, knew what she'd said, done; he spoke quickly, jumped into the gap, saving her embarrassment.

"Daisy, you'll really have to come and meet father ... soon."

"I'm really, *really* sorry, I didn't mean to speak as though he was ... in the past tense ... Really ..."

"It doesn't matter at all ... Now, it'll have to be today, this afternoon – can you manage that? We have to set off quite early, tomorrow ... long way ..."

"Yes, of course".

Only then, did Stuart remember what he'd long meant to ask her – but, as chance would have it, she, excitedly, got in first.

"Er ... just one thing ... A bit nosey of me, I suppose, but I'm dying to know ... to ask. What *actually* does Bill do? What's his ... occupation?"

"Oh, do you not know? Well, I'm sure I'm not divulging any confidence – he's an undertaker, funeral director".

"But ... the evening commitments, getting called out ...?"

"Oh, that's simple. His company, Pennoyre & Abel, like many funeral directors these days, offer a bereavement counselling service. And Bill does it for P & A. Yes, he's very able ..."

"So that's it! Yes quite, a natural when it comes to listening to people with problems, I can vouch for that from experience".

"Indeed, he's very much discovered his gift, and that not exactly early in life. He was telling me on the phone, a few nights ago, that he's going off to do further training, yes, got a place at Bristol for next year."

"Really? Splendid!"

"But he's much too modest to talk about it. Now, what we must do is arrange to meet after lunch – I've got to do some business at the bank – then we can go to Crowsavon together – about 2.30?"

"Fine. Where?"

"Let's say, by the lifeboat house, next to the church?"

"Right!"

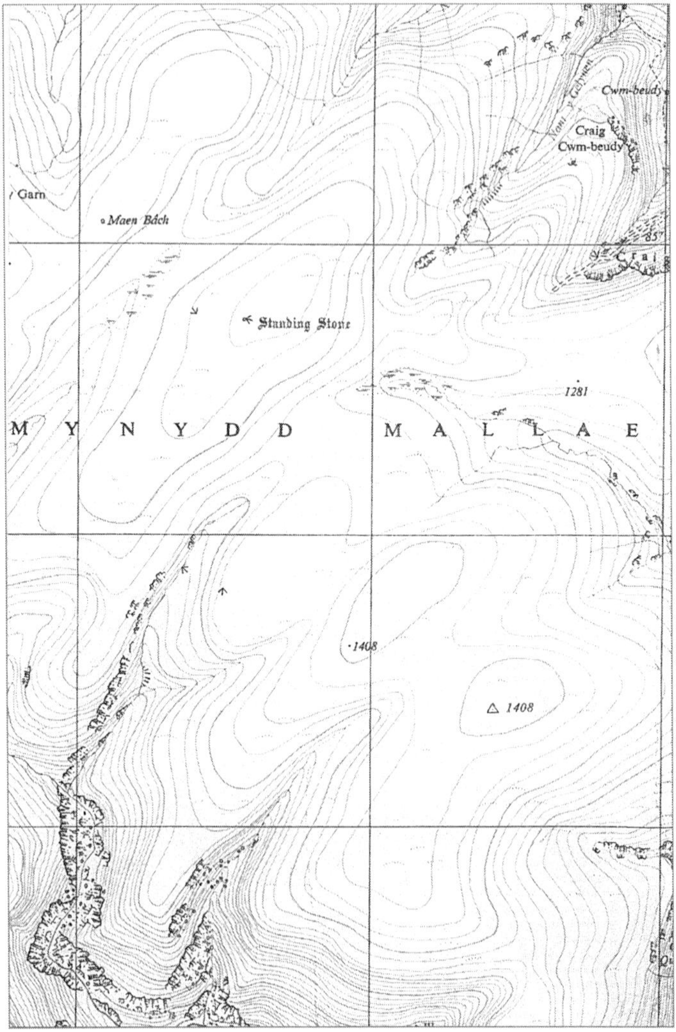
Cwm-beudy
Craig
Cwm-beudy
Garn
Maen Bâch
Standing Stone
1281
M Y N Y D D M A L L A E
1408
1408

It's curious, waking up on a mountain-side. For one thing, it takes a while to realise where you are ... nocturnal dreams of soft, secure beds still linger; then, also, you can wake thinking that the floor will be level! So, at first, a kind of dizziness or disorientation grips you; but not for long. In a while, you know you're here again ... in this place! That sounds like I consider it a curse – when I chose to come on this long trip – and first thing in the day, it's easy to get to thinking of it like that; the warmth of your bed – sleeping-bag or whatever – is not something you wish to quit. But then the smell of cooking breakfast drifts over you. Well, that's not correct, is it? – because often you yourself are the first up, and there's nothing there, nothing done, and so there's no nice smell until you've got to, and started producing it; but the point is that, when waking, emerging, into this emptiness – as it seems – I learned early to raise my spirits with this fabricated experience, this imagining, a promise to myself, that this – the real thing, that is – would come very soon. On this particular day, it's more necessary than ever to imagine the cooking bacon, because – well, no beating about the bush – it's dark, cold, and wet. And now I must get the stove going! No point waiting. Any of the others would not, and I would not also.

Later, back in my tent, sheltering as well as I can, the map tells me all it's able about our chosen route – well, the best that's left to us. The others are silent, their meal almost done, each with his own thoughts, as he packs and folds, rolls bedding and canvas. All of a sudden, I have an idea about that: whatever might be the purpose of carrying it all, the weight dragging us down, threatening to overbalance us, topple us over some unseen cliff, small perhaps, but well able to give a man a hard, disabling fall ... leave a man shattered, helpless, immobile on a drift of scree, the hard, cold rain seeping into his clothes, his body? But still we pack and carry it, help and load each other, as before, despite my thoughts; this is what such men as us do.

Last night, I was awake long, even towards morning. Through a hole in my tent – it's worn thin, so long relied on – I saw a full moon up above, the coldness of the night, and lack of cloud, causing it to swell almost, in my perception. It seemed to look down on me, knowingly, peering through my sharp mind, my thoughts expelled, cleared, by the stillness. I had the notion that the old moon breathed, gently – but, of course, it was the sound of one of the others, in a tent nearby. And I found myself thinking about what he might be dreaming of; but every man's dreams are silently his own, secure, their very existence hidden; but perhaps the moon knew mine.

The day's descent went well, initially, and though the rain drove hard against us, and each was goggled and wrapped, we quickly discovered a regular, persistent almost synchronised gait, tramping and trudging forever onward, to the valley below. Only the wind resisted us, at first; though soon we came upon very boggy, marshy land, a kind of place – perhaps there is some Welsh for it – that I have often noticed, where the rain gathers, trapped, and while no lake forms, neither does it seem to drain to the river below. In such places, of course, the chance of slipping, on the mud, is great, the hazard ever present. We passed through it unharmed, however, and soon our cause for cursing turned to a fresh slope of hard, sharp stones. Our idea was to work round a little to the east, and get down via Craig Rhosan, and by way of the bed of Nant Rhosan, which looked quite small, but had as surely gouged its way as the other, larger, streams. Yes, it looked as though it would be steep and rocky going, at first, but then quite manageable. As we approached it, more than once I looked back – and felt sure I saw signs of bad weather (well, worse; its was already drizzling) drawing down to us from the summit we had not long left, above. They were like grey fingers, and they ran, like the fingers of a hand, together, co-ordinated, down the small valleys into which the mountain split. It was though they were hurrying to reach us. As time passed, I looked back more and more; and became convinced – with dread – that they were the dark clouds, not of rain or light mist, but actual fog – the worst thing we could have dreamt of (men can walk in darkness, when the light of the moon is above them – I have read of this – but dense fog is most treacherous, because by that, you can see nothing, nothing; it means walking totally blind, and then it is very easy to step off a precipice, or tramp, for what will seem hours, if not actually be hours, towards some eminence beyond which there is actually no way down, no possible road beyond).

Each time I look round to check the dark fingers' encroachment, I am aware of something strange – or rather, not aware of it. I notice, each time, that someone seems to be missing (before I have felt abandoned, quite alone, but never, then, was I aware of actual absences; then, the simple count would never reveal it).

In the end, I discovered – with some horror, considering the swirling grey darkness (that seemed to reach forward, to us, faster) that the Craig Rhosan gap was just as treacherous as Craig-y-Rhaidr, and so, disappointed and dismayed, we set off back up the way we'd come, intending, now, to move further east, and then down into the cutting made by Afon Gwenlas. It would be exceedingly steep at first, but then, when we'd finally descended it, the very worst of today's journey would be over, as the Gwenlas sped easily down rapidly-softening landscape, towards meadows, where there were homesteads marked – and on, to the Tywi – and Crowsavon. Yes, there was no denying it, no avoidance; I could only see one other, now, and he seemed, at this moment at least, quite caught in a frightful thicket that I myself had skirted.

50

This time, Stuart had brought the car, as all sorts of provisions and goods were needed, so they'd met at the car park above Porthmeor. On the way there, they talked about various things.

"I thought … Er …" Stuart thought how best to put it.

"Yes?", she asked.

"About the book … I thought it best not to mention it … not just now …"

"Oh, I'm sure you're right."

"Maybe later, we can say how I found it amongst our things in Bromley – got mixed up with our papers, and we thought it a good idea to show it to you."

"Yes, I'm more than happy with that".

One thing he'd always found – Daisy was so easy going, happy to go along with any circumstances. After all, she could have been pressing to meet father some while ago, which might not have seemed, well, appropriate, then. When they sped through Carbis Bay, and on down the hill to Lelant (Stuart wondered why it was that the buses seemed to take so much longer – presumably it was all those stops) he could not help noticing the scenes where significant things had happened, or the pathways to them, recently or in the past; and he knew she had noticed them, thought about them, also. But there was no other way to go.

51

"My dear! You've come back to see me again, how nice, how very nice!"

Daisy didn't know what to make of the Robert Levenham's greeting. Was he at all what she'd thought? He appeared both aged and wiry, somewhat bent, but strong and fit; after all, he was actually only – what was it? Sixty-six. Perhaps this was how she knew he would appear, what she'd known to expect – and yet, people that you studied, read about, and thought about for a long time, were never quite the same on meeting. Crowsavon, also, wasn't quite what she'd expected inside. Stuart had tried to explain that it was a purpose-built care-home that had perhaps been built on a virgin site, but, despite its newness and functionalism, it was beautifully appointed, and had the very best facilities – sort of top-of-the-range, presumably, and, she realised, a bit more than Stuart and Rosemary could have afforded – this, at least, was the unspoken implication of his words.

"Yes, it's wonderful to see you again ... They tell me you're not a nurse any more, but ... but a ..."

"Dad, Daisy's an art historian. She's studying your work, particularly the paintings Bill has – remember Bill buying quite a lot ... and in the old days, too?

"Oh? Oh how interesting!"

"Daisy's *never been* a nurse", Rosemary chipped in, in reinforcement, "you're thinking of me, I'm a nurse".

"Oh, are you? Really? Well, that's a coincidence! That makes two of you!" Rosemary didn't bother trying to disabuse him. Actually, Daisy thought, he *did* seem to recognise me, think he'd seen me before.

"I thought you might like to show Daisy some of the drawings you have here?" Stuart acted to move things on, she noticed, more than once in the afternoon.

"O yes! Good idea!" – and he rifled in piles of papers, finally bringing out thick, dusty, pieces of cartridge, about two feet by one.

"Did you notice the suitcase by the door?" – whispered Rosemary to Daisy, as though in conspiracy – he's wanting to be off, shortly ... that's the way he is, poor love!"

"Some of these ... go back a *very* long way ...", said Robert to Daisy excitedly. Perhaps he would have shown them to Rosemary and Stuart, if they'd shown a lot of interest; she, Daisy knew, had been presented as someone with a special concern, extra knowledge, someone, as it were, within a community of knowledge of which the others were outsiders.

"Now, as an ... what was it? – art historian, you'll know about the Slade, won't you? The Slade school, at University College?"

"Oh yes".

"And you'll know about their tradition, their ... the emphasis on *life* studies. We all drew from life, you know ... that was the backbone ... actually, talking of backbones..." Robert showed her a drawing where the model was seen largely from behind, its *contrapposto* emphasising her spine as it curved gently round and up her back.

"And not a bad bottom, into the bargain, eh? Don't you think?"

"Dad!" Daisy couldn't work out if Rosemary was herself mildly shocked, or just shocked on behalf of their female visitor.

"Rosemary!" Robert addressed his daughter-in-law with pretend haughtiness. "This young woman knows about art and art schools, *she* has no problem with an artist's admiration of his model – do you my dear?". Daisy smiled.

"But ... the life-studies you did at the Slade ..."

"Yes?"

"As you say, the Slade's tradition, their ... philosophy of art education ... Mastery of the human form."

"Yes?"

"But ... you didn't really ... the human form does not figure in your work – as far as I know it."

"Well ... I suppose there are reasons for that ... I mean, once out on your own, you have to pay models ... all comes down to cost ... Now, the sea, the rocks, the sky ... they're always there ... free, *eternal* ... And ..." – now it was his turn to be conspiratorial – "*You have to keep models warm all the time ...*"

"Dad!" – Rosemary seemed genuinely disapproving.

"Let's have some tea, now. I bought some of that lovely saffron cake you can get in the town!" Stuart had changed their conversation's subject.

"Oh good!"; Robert, clearly, had a somewhat boyish appreciation of a tea party, and Rosemary knew that there was never more harmony among them all than when she was bustling round with tea cups and cakes. "Well, Dad, thank goodness you've never lost your appetite".

"*What?*" – he had become a little deaf, though.

When they'd eaten, and Robert assuaged his need of tea and cake, he made a point of getting out a framed panel that he'd kept beside his wardrobe. Daisy reckoned it would be about thirty by twenty centimetres.

"What d'you think of that?" Robert addressed only Daisy, denying, almost any sight of the panel to the others. The inner community of special knowledge, Daisy realised, was securely established, now – not that this fact gave her any ideas with which to answer.

"Well ... it's a very centrally-placed composition, I mean the subject ... It dominates because of its centrality ..." Robert nodded vigorously in the direction of his son and daughter-in-law; this visitor, that they had brought, indeed possessed real understanding, was the real thing.

"It does. So important, is the subject, that there's no possibility of it being presented in profile, or in any way allowing the eye to glance past it towards … And also, because of another, rather less intentional and purposeful motif, cause …"

"Er … yes?" Daisy was puzzled – what was she missing?

"It was done from a photograph, yes, can you not tell? The photographer composed it thus … he only saw the mountain … but the … *crucial* nature of the mountain … its *meaning* …"

"I can see – guess – that it's very important to *you* … you brought *this* picture with you here, this one, out of …"

"Yes, that's right. It's a mountain in Wales … I spent a long time looking at the photograph before I … I don't normally paint from such … *found*, existing images … No, I've never actually been there, of course … Mynydd … Mynydd … I know, nowadays you're not a nurse …you're one of those women with … a pad and pen, that's it! What is it? What's the word …? Take letters …If only I could think …"

"I think maybe … maybe we'd better be …" Stuart had suggested that the time would come when it might be best to take her back home. Of course, she'd wanted to ask his father about many things … *If all art's inspiration comes from … beyond … it must come from … Where?* She'd known, really, that the Robert she would be meeting would not be that of the paintings … or the book … Different – that's what she'd find, something different … *someone* different … Must be content, not disappointed. And now she'd look at human forms differently, in his work, look *for* them … if she got the chance …"

"No … look, I'll get myself back to St. Ives".

"Look, it'll only take …"

"No, I will. You've got a lot to do – off early tomorrow. I'll get a bus, or walk". She made clear that she would not be dissuaded.

"Well, if you're really *sure*."

"Well my dear", said Robert, seeing that she was going, "it's been so lovely to see you – and, please, don't leave it so long, next time!" Daisy said goodbye to him, and Stuart walked her to the front door.

"While I think of it ... mustn't forget again ... there's just one thing I keep meaning to ask you ..."

52

"Even stars go out, die,
yes, one by one their light we see no more,
and over all of us, silently, there is a kind of blackness,
made, created by, the light that <u>was</u>
– remembered only, now, no longer real, just imagined.
But I thought to ask myself what kind of light or darkness there would have been
– or other thing – beyond and before any being at all?
No vacuous holes or absences, were ever made by never-was-ness.
There must be innocence of any guilt whatever, for those which never were at all;
the guilt, held for them, must accrue to those others,
who cruelly chose to choose that they not be.
But now there are bright, white flowers in the green vastness;
and beyond it – further than eye can see – blueness, true eternity."

A tear formed in Daisy's eye, as she read Robert's words, in the book, that night. Those words went with the painting he gave to Clive, of course – *Innocence*. She knew what it meant.

53

Next day, a letter arrived for her:

My dear Daisy,
   Just one thing – it only occurred to me as I was driving home; I didn't want to talk on the phone about this – perhaps, in this respect, the old ways really are the best, well, the most secure.
   There's one thing that I might have mentioned, if I'd thought about it last week, that you might want to know. I think, looking back, that one

reason Clive might have put his hydralysg on the back burner, so to speak, is that he seemed to have come to the conclusion – judging by one or two comments that I've now remembered him coming out with – that it could have a pathological (indeed, necrotic) effect on certain brain cells, leading to a partial degenerative effect. I realise, from what you've told me, that this has great implications for his bother's condition. Obviously, that possible conclusion is a guess, and may not be relevant at all – but if it is … I thought you'd want to know about this.

From what you said, I imagine you'll be back home in the next few weeks, when I'll look forward to exploring it further. By then, I might just have remembered more about what Clive said concerning hydralysg.

Love,
Mum.

54

"Miss Taylor? Can I talk with you? Is it convenient?"

It was mid-morning. Bill was off burying the dead or consoling the bereaved, presumably, and there was this smartly-dressed, yet casual, young woman at the door; Daisy's generation, but a few years' older, she thought. Then, she realised who she was. "Can I … come in?" Daisy muttered something, and showed the visitor in to the front sitting room, which Bill had urged her to use whenever she felt the need ("The parents kept it 'strictly for best' for thirty years – didn't use it, that is. I don't intend to do the same"). She took off her coat, and sat (intentionally?) with her back to the bay-window, the light behind her.

"Yes, it was me, the other night. And yes, let me say, I *was* just giving Mitch a run across Porthgwidden beach, and then …"

"You found me?"

"No, not I. Mitch did. You were totally invisible to me – the twilight."

"Well, many, *many* thanks … for …"

"I say I was just walking the dog. Please let me assure you ... it was a coincidence that I was there, purely."

"Why ...? Why ever should it not be?"

"You don't ... don't otherwise recognise me?"

"No! Should I?"

"Well, having come back with you, that night ..."

"*Helped* me back – without you ..."

"Having come here, seen where you live *now* ... I plucked up the courage to ... try to visit you, talk ..."

"What ... is this?"

"It was a few months ago, now, and you would have seen me ... very briefly".

Daisy looked more closely, strained forward to find a better view. At last she had an inkling.

"My name is Lucy Charlton. I work ..."

"*Secretary* ... Thingy & Wotsit!"

"Mr. Turley's secretary, yes. I live in the town, here ... travel to Truro each day ... a few days' off, at the moment ..."

"And ... your visit ...?"

"It's ...er ... about Robert Levenham ..."

"*Robert?* You know him?"

"Indeed. I ... got to know him ... very well ..."

"Here in St. Ives ... or ...?"

"No. Let me explain. For most of my career, I was a nurse, geriatric, mainly. I got to know Mr. Levenham when I worked at Crowsavon – the care home by Lelant – I think you know it?"

"Yes, indeed. I visited ..."

"Yes. Often the residents ... well, make a friend of a particular nurse or carer ... show them their family photographs and the like."

"Oh ...?"

"But with Robert it was much more. He needed a friend, or rather, a friend that was a young woman of ... our age. No, I don't mean in the way people would suppose ... his need – if that isn't too strong, was for ..."

"A daughter. Rose – whose death was as real to him ..."

"You know about Rose? She's buried in Carbis Bay – there's a cemetery there. Of course, she would have been rather older then me, but ... And he loved someone to share his work with, his art."

"Really?"

"I didn't get to see many of his paintings – he only has four at Crowsavon – but he has piles of drawings and etchings ..."

"I only got to see a few of those."

"He would tell me about ... well, everything. His work, as I've said, his family, his student days in London ..."

"He remembers a lot about that? The early days?"

"Yes – geriatric memory can be a strange thing ... And of course, there is his ... condition ... He wanted to paint me – we had created a studio for him, not big but ..."

"Yes, I was told."

"And he did – paint me, I mean. Well, one thing and another, and the management at Crowsavon didn't think too much of it. You'll realise that there is always the possibility, in geriatric care, of nurses and staff ... abusing such friendship, always the risk of care-homes employing, er ..."

"Gold-diggers?"

"Well ... quite. With Robert, his condition was quite advanced, such that there was much, clearly, that had happened in his past – significant things – that he had no knowledge of. Well, inevitably, someone of his age has had many ... but much of it had gone. However, he had clearly written a lot down."

"Yes?" Daisy had a curious feeling, knew where this was heading ...

"He had obviously written a diary, written down many things. He talked often about 'the book', 'It's all in the book!' – he would say ... as though ... as though an old, sick person could let his memory just sleep, fade, and everything significant he had done and ... everything important to him ... would be recorded somewhere, set safe in some place beyond any hazards or ... accidents of the present – or where he might be now, *how* he might be ... so – the book!"

"So – you left Crowsavon?"

"And nursing and healthcare, yes. I re-trained as a secretary."

"Of course! Woman with a pencil and a pad ... *secretary*, the lost word! I'm sorry. When I went, with Stuart, to see his father, recently, he kept talking about a nurse, who was no longer a nurse – he'd heard – but was now one of those 'women with a pen and pad' – he'd forgotten the word."

"So he asked about me? How pleasant! I left Crowsavon a few years ago – late '90s – but he remembers ... Well, after a while I specialised in legal work, and so got a job with Mr. Turley. I discovered that he had become solicitor to Professor Levenham – Robert's brother – soon after he came to Cornwall, not long before I started there. Then one day, we heard of Professor Levenham's sudden death, and shortly after that, what should come to the office but a letter ... from a university teacher, seeking an introduction to Robert Levenham's family ..." This, Daisy realised – feeling distinctly queasy, now – was where she came into it.

"This person – you – came to interest me more and more ... particularly as the letter was written from a house in the next street to mine."

"You live ...?"

"Yes ... and I know those houses, where you had a flat, quite well. I got to thinking that *there*, only a stone's thrown away, was a girl who was very interested in Robert and ... I thought of, well, coming to introduce myself ... tell you what I knew."

"And did you ... come round? Was I out?"

"I went up the street once or twice, just to look, to be certain ... Then, I got to thinking, 'That's where this Miss Taylor lives'"

"Did you ...venture in, as it were ...?"

"I went up the Digey one day, for another reason entirely, and I thought to go past your flat ... and what should I see but a dark, middle-aged woman coming from the alley at the *back* of the property – and she had a very strange look on her face ... clearly, something was not right ... as though she'd just been caught doing something ... well ... She certainly scuttled off fast ... And, immediately, I thought, *She looks vaguely familiar*. Only much later did I realise who she might be, where I'd probably seen her – she'd have come in to the office to sign documents, surely, when Professor Levenham died. Anyway, I thought just to peep in, and see where she'd come from …A strange exit, undoubtedly, from Miss Taylor's abode …"

"And so … so you got into my flat …?"

"I didn't even need to open an unlocked door … I was in before I was aware of it."

"And you damaged my books and papers." A certain sparkle, fire, had lit her eyes, at moments in her story; but now, Lucy Charlton seemed deflated.

"I became sure, certain, that you had Robert's book, among all those … things … Then I saw that strange note, that had been left to you … wondered what it might mean. Clearly someone thought you were not quite who you claimed – maybe they were right … and then it was *I* who seemed to appear like a … gold-digger … The note made me … I suppose I'd say … what is it the criminals claim? Red mist appearing over the eyes? Of *course* you didn't have Robert's book, how might you have done? What I did was … just wrong, *unforgiveable* …" By this time, Lucy Charlton was close to breaking down. *Well, two intruders in the same place, in the same hour, and both filled with remorse! Not quite what you expect from burglars … better I suppose, though, this way …*

"Can I get you some tea or something?", Daisy asked, but before Lucy could respond said: "He thought I was *you* … Robert thought I was a former-nurse. He asked me why I'd taken so long to visit him, 'Do come again, and don't leave it so long next time' – that sort of thing. Would the Crowsavon staff let you in to see him? How was your leaving, your break with the place?"

"I'm just … just so *sorry* …"

"No, no …"

"I just had to … try to see you – once I knew where you were, after … that night."

"*Go and see him* … It's what he'd want …"

55

Well it wouldn't have done any good! The book, of course had been lying on Daisy's desk, a floor above where they had been sitting. But telling her about it, showing it to her ... that would just have led to ... problems, Daisy reasoned. *I've recently become quite used to suppressing information!* At least, she thought, she didn't actually *deny* that she had it ... In fact, she wouldn't have it for much longer ... She'd reached the end, but for a transcribed scene from *The Tempest*, and she'd phoned Stella – a little nervously at first – and told her about having talked about it to Robert; and she arranged that she should take it to him, in London ... where she was returning soon. Stella seemed happy with that plan. Daisy did not tell her about the hydralysg discovery. Clive's possible part – though Daisy felt certain of it – in Robert's mental decline was perhaps best not shared; if it had been, then Stella would feel wrong-footed, aggrieved again. She'd copied extensively from the book, by hand – spreading it out over a photocopier at the public library or somewhere had not seemed an appropriate option, she'd thought. If she did need to use it again, she felt sure Stuart would oblige. But ... use it again? How should she proceed ...? If ...? What next? What – if anything – *now*? No, the book's *actua*l final words – a sort of epitaph, signing-off – were:

"Concerning those things which we cannot speak, We must perforce keep silent."

Perhaps there might always be – surely would be – things of every person's life, hidden, kept silent.

56

The waiter behaved as though he knew them, recognised her from the last visit; but probably that was how they learned to behave, a kind of professional manner (Daisy fantasised about Waiter School, in which the students practised a polished table-side manner, and Continental accents). As she said to him, this was the very least she could do, he'd done so much for her, and tonight, Bill must choose whatever he liked, and had to cook nothing.

"But ..." She was lost for the right words. "Your ...work – it's amazing!"

"Not really ... I just discovered ...You know how it is – I'm sure you do – when you simply *know* this is what you can do, *should* be doing ..."

"Well, I like to think I'm good at what I try to do ... and also this research business ..."

"I'm sure you are."

"Well, on the writing and publishing, we have yet to see."

"I realised, the other night, that you were having doubts."

"I seem to have discovered that ... when you enquire very closely, deeply, into, well, an artist, or it might be a writer, whatever ... you sometimes end up finding out ... things about *yourself*. It can't always be, well, quite like my present experience, but ..."

"What's that ancient Greek thing, 'Know Thyself'?"

"Well, for me it's been a bit of a ... baptism of fire." Their main courses were arriving. More deferential beaming from the waiter. "I've been thinking ..."

"Yes?"

"I think I might not ask Mum about ... you know, Clive's idea ... termination."

"No?"

"Well, she also has gone through it ... with my discovering my paternity, and about Clive ... her relationship ...and ..."

"Yes?"

"We've always got on so well ... been so close – just being the two of us."

"And ... why jeopardise ...?"

"Robert seemed certain that there'd been no chance that she'd needed to be influenced by him. Maybe I was always secure ... So I might say nothing – at least for a long while."

"Increasingly, as time goes on, there will be people such as yourself, who will learn that ... that they only *are* by chance ...We hear, from time to time, about ... survivors of hideous procedures ... intended to end ..."

"Though, I've already confided to you, and Stuart ... I've never to talked to her, the person most concerned, closest to me ..."

"Closeness does not *always* require complete disclosure of everything – sometimes the opposite. Sometimes silence, and discretion, cements the seal of ... well, caring, intimacy ..."

"How very well put ... beautiful ..." *And to think – he was, till recently, just a country-town undertaker ...* "I'm not certain though ... might change my mind."

"Of course."

This time, Daisy decided, she was *definitely* going to order a sweet ... crème brûlée, perhaps, that *had* been on the menu.

57

Faster and faster the hills and fields went by, and more and more the wildness receded, the rugged land being replaced, quite perceptibly, with gentle landscape. Why was it, Daisy wondered, that whenever the Cornish landscape – outcrops of rocks, white mounds of clay, and the sudden plunging of the land into valleys beneath thin-legged viaducts – had been changed to tidy meadows and lanes, the train seemed to go faster, seemed to sense that now the strenuous part was over, and it might press easily onward through somnolent West Country shires, towards busy Home Counties, that were crossed with a skein of feverish motorways?

You wanted to know – and I'm sorry I asked you if I might explain later, causing you yet more waiting – about what started me off on this; well ...

"Drinks Madam? Any drinks, sandwiches, snacks, cakes ...?" A uniformed man pushing a trolley raucously interrupted her thoughts, her plan of exactly how to put it, get it down. Returning the book by recorded post would give her an opportunity to write to Stuart about various things.

"No, thank you."

First, though, I do want to report something that I found out the other day, from Mum. She says that, on several occasions, Clive suggested that one possible result of hydralysg was its effect on the brain, and ... No, that won't do ...

- But first, let me pass on something I discovered recently. It seems likely ... probable that your father became adversely affected by his brother's drug ... No ...

- Since the day we met in St. Ives, and I came to Crowsavon, another possibility, regarding the effect of this hydralysg, upon your father, has come to light. I had a letter from my mother, who'd remembered ... In the end, Daisy wasn't certain how she'd put it, what would be the best way.

What first put me on to your father's work? Well, I'd become very interested in British Realist painters some while back, particularly those who clung to the development of that tradition long after "mainstream" or official art had rejected realist depiction, and veered away down ... Then, one day (I was to discover, later, that this was not very long after Clive had died), I received a letter, or package. It was sent to the Department, where I work; it was quite a surprise. It was various cuttings – photocopied, some of them – from local papers eg. St. Ives Times & Echo, etc., with articles about this interesting local painter who, unlike the better-known St. Ives artists (avant gardists like Hepworth and Nicholson, etc.) was keeping alive a long-established local tradition that was now much scorned, particularly by the establishment ... Several of the cuttings were from the time of the exhibition you mentioned to me, at the Society of Artists. Many of them had been highlighted with a red highlighter pen – particularly a phrase about "It's about time Robert Levenham received proper attention ..." and "Where is the critic or academic who will give this man his due?" That was a challenge to me, as it was, without the red pen. But these had been sent to me with a purpose – and soon after I received it, I asked around in the office, and, apparently, a while back, a mystery caller had been asking about the teaching staff, and their various research interests ... and he (it was a man) had mentioned my name. So, I had been put on to Robert Levenham intentionally. Of course, I've wondered many times about it, talked to Mum, and – as suggested – done a lot of asking around at the University.

Now – as she'd got into her stride with this mental letter-writing (it was no longer just planning) – she'd begun to wish she had paper and pen ... and began scrabbling in her bulging, chaotic handbag ... to no avail.

What I think, what I've decided, finally, is that <u>Clive</u> sent the package. Finding where I worked, and ascertaining my particular interests, was easy. The postmark was too smudged to be useful – but I bet it was Truro, or at least somewhere in Cornwall. Had he arranged for Turley to send it, in the event of his death? She'd had an opportunity to try to find the answer to that one recently ... Lucy Charlton was sure to have known ... Perhaps she should have quizzed her? ... Should she tell Stuart about Lucy? About the other intruder? ... *Or maybe he'd made some informal arrangement in Mevagissey; I realise that if <u>this</u> latter was the case, it suggests he knew that some fatal condition hovered over him. But, if it was an instruction to Turley, it might have been more open-ended.*

You're thinking: why should Clive have done all this, gone to all this trouble? For what purpose? Thinking of all the possibilities, I came to the conclusion that Clive definitely wanted everything to be discovered, and that he was <u>surely</u> the sender (and who else might be?). And all I subsequently found out fitted in with this. Another thing Stella said to me, that day we met: "As time went by, my husband increasingly needed pardoning and forgiveness" – or words to that effect. Yes, he <u>wanted</u> to be exposed. Perhaps he'd thought of the possibility – intended? – that my receipt of the information would get me talking about the Levenham family, eg. to Mum, who might reveal his own ... role in my existence (as happened).

You asked me once about the book – or rather, suggested that I might discover how it had come to be with Clive's papers (and this from his London days). Well, I can't say I've been successful on that one, though

I suppose I still might. We know Robert was well aware of its existence, when he was first at Crowsavon ... Oh dear – I really will have to tell him about Lucy, if I put this bit in ... *When I was walking to the station, this morning, I'd just left the house (Bill, I must say, has been just wonderful!) when something struck me. Only the day before, I'd been reading the last parts of the book. In the last entry (except a few final words) he'd transcribed a scene from a Shakespeare play, The Tempest (I didn't think much of this, the book is full of quotations, large and small, from all kinds of sources). But, wheeling my suitcase down from Bill's, I thought to stop into that second-hand book shop just off the High Street. I got a cheap battered school text of The Tempest. The scene Robert had copied was that in which Prospero, the magician and former-ruler who has been exiled on the island, throws away his book (from which his spells etc. have come) to a place where he can never again retrieve it. Now Robert's book was not the source of his power or magic, rather it was the place in which he examined his own soul (through various media), and in which he told us – if we were to find it – about his relationship with us, and ours with one another. The place he cast it – not to be retrieved by him, since he was to be held fast in his ... condition – was into the keeping of ... the man who had put him there, who really did – if all these guesses of mine are right – want to be totally exposed, found out. Clive did want to atone for what he'd done, I'm convinced, thus, he revealed his guilt regarding me, and my mother; and also, he'd done his best for Robert in organising good health care, and paying for it – and ensuring that this would continue (after his own death) as long as it was needed.*

"Can I have your attention please? The buffet shop will be closing in half an hour ... half an hour"; the crackly voice, from somewhere above, jolted Daisy back to reality. Soon they'd be racing through Surrey ... then Waterloo ... and the struggle down to the Underground. She wondered if she'd got change for the machines ... or would she have to queue? More groping in her bag followed.

Did Clive want us to know about the book, see it? Who can tell.
She knew she'd be too tired, tonight, actually to write ... must do it tomorrow, though.

Bill made an interesting suggestion: many successful, important, men – particularly those who rise high early in life – tend to be … have a certain moral … blindness, at first … but then, later, come to question everything that has, so easily, come to them – and with this can come, well, realization of things they have done wrong to others – guilt. As Stella suggested, at that stage of his life, I think the main concern of … my father (I must call him who he was) was making up for things … making things right. Later, perhaps I'll contact her again, see if I can go down and … find out more about him …

58

"Er … Daisy? Daisy Taylor? Darren here – Darren Scott?"

"Oh, hello Darren."

"Er, it's about Freddie – Freddie Jackson? I told him I'd give you a ring."

"Oh …"

"Yes, he was really hoping to see you?"

"Well, I only got back from Cornwall yesterday – and there's so much to do … the flat …"

"Well, thing is … he's had an accident … slipped on something … fell down the stairs?"

"Bacon!"

"No, slipped – the stairs? Not anything to do with … what he's eaten … Oh! Right! His cat! Yes, very likely! And all those papers and things he keeps there?"

"Quite. How is he? Badly hurt?"

"Damaged his … coccyx? No, really – last bone of the spine".

"Yes, I know."

"Well, he didn't want to call you … cause bother … but he'd really like … And I said, look, I'm going to ring her …"

"So … is he at home, or hospital, or …?"

"Oh, home. Bed downstairs. Social services … really good people!"

"Darren, tell him I'll be over on Thursday … just *got* to get some paperwork out of the way, first … bills, letters …"

59

"I've been a very bad man – and stupid into the bargain!" Well, Daisy had to admit to the latter, if that meant storing papers on the stairs, and believing accidents only happened to other people.

"You see ... I wasn't quite ... well, I never told you the *whole* truth ... I did so like ... your visit ... I'd got to thinking how nice it would be ... time to time ... share my Earl Grey with ... a very, *very* lovely young woman – can I call you that? You'll get to thinking I'm just another dirty old man – as well as deceitful!".

"Freddie, take it easy! I can tell you're in much ...well, discomfort. There's plenty of time to tell me about ... whatever it is. And just why should it *have* to be unpleasant, that an elderly man likes to have young people around."

"Rebecca ... she used to run up and down the stairs – no papers there then. That was ... that was ... Oh, youth!"

"Has she ... not been in touch ... recently ...?"

"Levenham! Let's not ... I must tell ... I told the truth when I said I did not know him, know Robert Levenham. But we knew *Clive* Levenham".

"*Clive?* The scientist?"

"Oh yes. Rachel must surely have told him all about ... her father, that is. Well, Bernie was very angry – things, then, were still not quite like they are today, not with – that sort of thing."

"You mean ...?"

"You were ... Levenham's child, of course you were. Bernie said 'That wretched man's got my daughter pregnant! Just when her career was about to take off!' You see, Bernie doted on Rachel, your mother, she was going to do all the things he'd wanted to do."

"But ... but Bernie was very good at what he did, successful."

"Yes, he was, but that took a while ... And what he'd really always wanted was an education, a *scientific* education. And this selfish young man had come along and ... Well, upshot was that Bernie was livid with ... your father, protested. Clive agreed to come round to the shop – I remember it well; it was Derby Day – he wanted, I suppose to talk him round, get him to see that ... it takes two to tango – if you don't mind ... I remember him being very struck by a few items we'd got in at the time. One was an awful thing by a young student (Bernie always thought he had to, er, help the young). 'Looks like he's been on drugs!' – I said. Actually, the thing – though awful – was awaiting collection; it'd sold easily, but the student, or whoever he was, had moved on. 'Yes, we could do with a few more like that!', Bernie said, probably not really meaning it; but Clive said he might just be able to help ... And that was how it started!"

Daisy groaned.

"So you did know ... about Clive's brother? Robert, the painter?

"My dear, when I said, before, that I didn't know him, or *of* him, that was absolutely the truth ... And you must remember, this man Clive didn't come up with anything ... for a few years. We forgot all about it."

"Er, 'Then one day' – you're going to say? You got a visit?"

"We didn't enquire where they came from."

Daisy groaned again, rose, and walked around the room, the collection of Leach pots and bronzes seeming quite put out by having to accommodate the clutter of bedding, a walking-frame, and an NHS commode on wheels.

"Could we have some ... tea?", Freddie asked, thinly, as though hoping to take from her mind the cloud that seemed to him to have descended on it. She found her way to the kitchen, and as she filled the kettle, Bacon came from nowhere, and rubbed his flank against her legs.

"Darren's off, today", he said, when Daisy returned, "some sort of works' outing ... New York. Yes, certainly a young man bound for good things – but got something solid behind him, unlike many of those City types ... qualifications, a profession ..."

"I fancy what you're saying is he's 'Quite a catch!'"

"Er ... yes". Freddie began to exhibit more colour than she'd seen so far that day. "So, it was Clive's brother Robert, who was producing the paintings?" No doubt he'd thought it best to steer the conversation back to art. "Well, they certainly appreciated his work in the Far East ... Went down a bomb in Nagasaki – Oh dear, I don't think I should have said that, should I? I don't seem ... today ... to be able to say anything right!"

"They don't have one at the Tate Modern, by the way."

"No?". Daisy could have sworn Freddie had a sheepish look.

"No. One possibility is that they began to ... have doubts about it, removed it ... "

"Or that you ... were sent on a fool's errand?" A lot of remorse followed. Daisy felt reluctant to mention the proceeds of the sales ... how much had been returned to Robert; there suddenly didn't seem any point.

"You will ... return? See us again? I know Darren would want that – and Bacon *certainly* would. Oh – I almost forgot – should the Titus hanging in the cloakroom be of use, please take it ... you'll find some brown paper wedged down beside the kitchen cupboard. Don't want all those eyes on it, in the train."

60

"Well I'll be blowed!"

Stuart just couldn't believe it. He re-read the relevant part of Daisy's longish letter again.

"You know, she's come to the belief – Rachel put her on to it – that Dad's condition was actually *caused* by this ... this drug of Clive's! ... Or at least, exacerbated ... Apparently, in the short term it's alright, but in the long term ... kills brain cells ..."

"Really?"

"Yes ... leads to ... well .."

"Right."

"You don't seem surprised?" Stuart couldn't understand why Rosemary wasn't as amazed as he was.

"Well, I'm not."

"*No?*"

"No. Obviously, I knew nothing about this ... substance, until you told me ... but ... once I *did* know ..."

"What?"

"Stuart, I've seen many dementia patients, and heard – professionally I mean – of others ... and Dad ..."

"What?"

"Well, I couldn't put my finger on it – now, like then – but ... he always seemed different, somehow ..."

"Well, I'll be blowed!"

"So you keep saying." Stuart returned to the letter:

Well, I haven't quite made up my mind yet, about talking to Mum – I might, I might not – so I'll have to ask for your confidence on – you know – indefinitely.

And then there's the big question of my – how shall I put it? – future work. I owe it to Robert to finish it, and publish something ... but as for my planned PhD – maybe one should find a research topic one's detached from. If this were a legal case or something, I'd have to declare a personal interest and retire. Anyway – here, as promised, is Robert's book. The most important thing, I think, is all his beautiful thoughts, or rather, his thoughts about beauty, truth, and goodness. They are truly spiritual, I think. No, it's not wrong to use the past tense; the Robert of these lines is no more – but I consider that all that he was, and believed, and felt – they are safe and secure, somewhere we do not know of, and nothing can negate them, now.

Stuart felt ... he couldn't think how to describe it ...

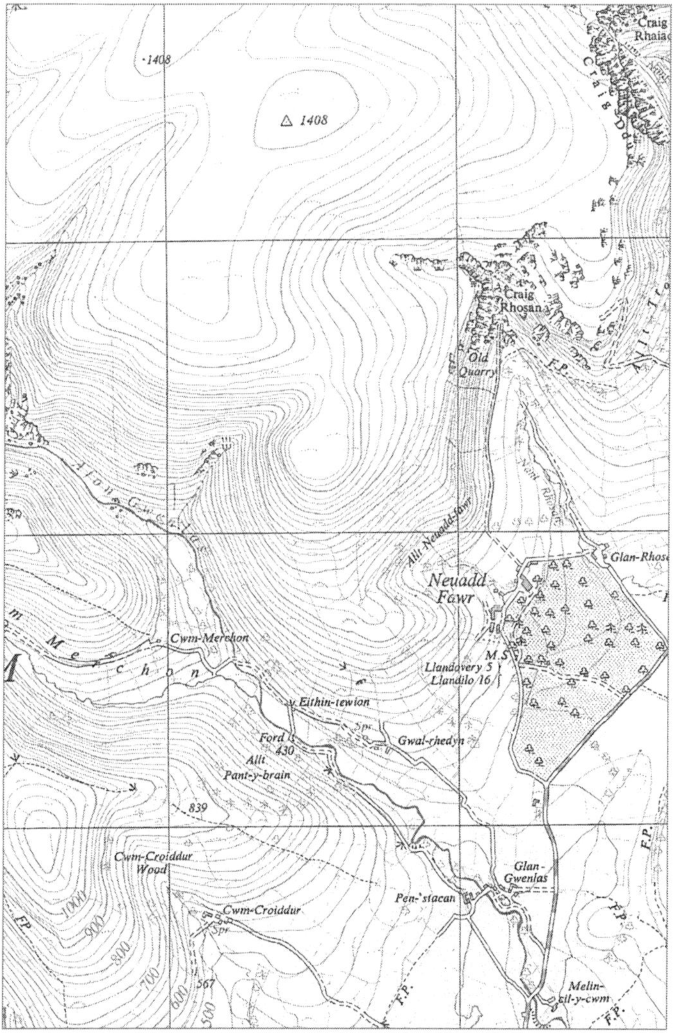
Craig
Rhaiad
Craig Ddu
1408
△ 1408
Craig
Rhosan
Old
Quarry
F.P.
Afon Gwenlas
Allt Neuadd-fawr
Nant Rhosan
Glan-Rhosan
Neuadd
Fawr
Cwm-Merchon
M.S.
Llandovery 5
Llandilo 16
y Eithin-tewion
Spr.
Gwal-rhedyn
Ford
430
Allt
Pant-y-brain
839
Cwm-Croiddur
Wood
Glan-
Gwenlas
Pen-stacan
Cwm-Croiddur
Spr.
1000
900
800
700
600
500
567
F.P.
Melin-
cil-y-cwm
F.P.

The ever-flattening landscape proved its promised charms, and before long even the thick tussocks and sheep-worn paths – some too thin to be useable – were disappearing. Now, it was a simple hike – with stick in hand, measuring out each yard, making each footstep sound, regular. And imperceptibly those feet were flattening out, not twisting upward to meet the gradient. Only the hill of Cae'r Beili had to be walked up, and down again, before the open moorland, unfenced grazing, met hedges, enclosure, and the graggy, slanting stones of enmeshed walling, through which delicate flowers would cling. I was home now, well nearly, as a few miles of this grassland would bring me to the river. But I was very weary.

It was as though the pack on my poor back had got heavier, more and more so, as the terrain had lain down, for although the end was in sight, and my spirits raised somewhat, in a different way, each step was heavier – different from the simplified business of moving on this gentle earth. Ahead, I knew my end, objective, would be waiting, almost – perhaps – in sight. Indeed, my eyes strained forward, peering up ahead, deciding, maybe, that here, *or* there *– beyond the thickets, between the trees' thick boughs, there would be Crowsavon, waiting. And with my head ever upwards, my eyes to the goal, I walked on – though, as I say, with a heavy burden.*

My eyes were so upward, to the fore, my thoughts only for the objective, that I was almost quite deceived, blinded – I failed to see the river, almost at my feet, under me; it had come to me almost before my realisation of it. But perhaps it needs must be thus, for I knew, strongly at that moment, that it would ever be avoided – perhaps the whole enterprise – if one had known it, known of it, known of a choice ... understood all of it, not just its coming. But it had to be crossed. I looked to right and left. There was no bridge or ford! Peering into the distance – east or west – was likewise useless. It had to be negotiated; this, and this only, was the way. It almost drew me into itself ... yes, it did – no time, then, for choosing ... it seemed my very feet slid down into its muddy banks, the precipitous sides sliding up to me, almost. I had one moment, only, to look around, just one moment ... to confirm my solitude, my fears ... and then the waters closed on me, shocked me.

I had not thought the Twyi could be so deep ... for its swirling dragged me down, suffocated me. I had not thought such darkness lay in its depths, for I felt every part of me drawn down, my eyes closed over ... such that I saw nought again, no more aware, conscious, by way of that vigilant sense, the one that had kept me so safe on the precipitous mountain; here, it was as nothing, gone. Oh, the coldness! For I had never thought the water would be so cold ... its chaos shatter me ... appal ...Then I felt a scrabbling at my feet, clawing, dragging ... I struggled, writhed... Finally, all my energy, my last strength, freed them. And alone ... but I had not thought! ... I was not, actually, alone ... for the Voice ... Still I thrashed at the waters, with almost all my striving futile – well, the lot. But would it last for ever, this struggle? This darkness? I was – perhaps – moving onwards, through ... not just consigned ever to stay in this dark place.

The shore was not as I'd anticipated, assumed ... for I had, indeed, reached it ... not guessing, thinking, that this, here, was it ... I quite thought I was naked, or at least, emptied of all I had carried; and beneath my soft feet, the grass inviting. Forward, I ran. This, all, was nothing such as I had imagined. Above, a shining light sparkled, sprayed at me (from where I couldn't see); so much light – it became – that I could see nothing, was blinded, momentarily (darkness was done with, there was no more rain). But I knew to walk on, ever forward (the Voice ...). Finally – I wept, let my tired, vanquished arms fall at my side – there was the pretty house! *The sharp-pointed gables sprang up on every side, the lacy barge-boards seemed rippling in the light, and the tall oversailing chimneys scraped the sky ... and from the entrance, the sound I had heard rang without quaver. Crowsavon, at last ... this was truly it ... And on the grass, flowers grew, and by the door, white and red.*

61

"*I can't get to the phone at present ... Please leave a message ...*"

"Oh ... er ... Stuart here. Daisy? Stuart. Yes, er ... I just thought you'd like to know ... well, not *like* ... but ... I got a call from Crowsavon last night ... yes ... It seems they found Dad ... er, died in his sleep, so they said. Found him this morning ... yes ... The nurse, whoever, who found him, said ... said she'd never seen someone looking as peaceful ... peaceful ... Well, that's wonderful, isn't it? Well, just thought I should tell you. Hope all's well ...do keep in touch ..."